CRAVE

OFF-LIMITS #1

PIPER LAWSON

PIPER LAWSON BOOKS

Content editing by Becca Mysoor
Line and copy editing by Erica Russikoff
Cover photography by Regina Wamba

Crave (verb):

To long for; want greatly; desire eagerly.

1

───────

OLIVIA

Gravel scrapes the soles of my Louboutins as I trip across the parking lot in the dark.

"The shoes are fucking hot," Kat says.

"They're not rated for off-roading." I send up a silent prayer for forgiveness as I dodge the empty beer cans and my roommate laughs.

The sign on the single-floor building in the middle of nowhere says "Velvet" in pink neon. The glow lingers in the corner of my vision when my friends line up at the bouncer, whose eyes have been on us since I was halfway across the lot.

He glances at Kat's ID, then Jules', but frowns at mine. "I don't think so, sweetheart. You're drunk."

"I'm the designated driver. I haven't had anything harder than soda tonight. You try walking across gravel in these."

"Yeah, I don't think so."

"I'm better behaved than anyone in there," I insist. "Not my fault these shoes were designed with smooth surfaces in mind."

He stares at me like I'm nuts. We're running low on options.

I look around, assuring myself there's no one else watching. "Fine. Would a drunk person be able to do this?"

I reach for my shoe and bend my knee, pulling my foot up to the apex of my thighs. Then I take a breath and lift it higher, straightening my leg so it's extended alongside my upper body.

His eyes round. He might've snuck a peek or two at the strippers who work the stage, but I've got moves he's never seen.

Releasing my leg, I grab my ID out of his hands and follow my friends inside.

"That was badass. Where have you been hiding that?" Kat shouts over the music as we head inside.

"Don't worry about it," I toss back. "Tonight's about celebrating your birthday and living life like a normal"—a glance back at the bouncer, grateful he didn't notice or care that our licenses were fake—"twenty-one-year-old."

I reach into my bag to pull out the Queen B tiara, and my roommate's eyes light up.

Kat's been bugging us for the past year to visit a part of town that's the opposite of the one starring in the glossy university recruitment brochures.

My corporate father and socialite mother would lose their shit if they saw me in a place like this. But we're here for Kat, and as much as this isn't a place I'd choose to spend my night, it's not about me. It's about friendship.

Kat sets the crown in her dark hair and tugs us toward the bar. There's no point trying to score a booth around the perimeter since Velvet is full. We wedge in, Jules calling for vodka sodas for her and Kat, and a Diet Coke for me.

On stage is a woman who looks too beautiful for this place. She winds around the pole, shifting toward the edge of the stage to drop her hips into a seductive slide.

A piece of hair escapes my tidy top knot to tickle my neck, but as I reach up to tuck it back in, I realize there's no runaway hair. Only a bead of sweat.

When the dancer finishes, a woman dressed

in a black T-shirt with the Velvet logo claims the mic.

"Shh, this is it," Kat breathes, and I arch a brow.

"This is what?"

"Amateur night!"

"You're not going up," I say, horrified.

Kat grins. "The prize is five hundred bucks. That's a hell of a birthday present."

She brushes off her hands and joins the throng of girls by the register, returning a few minutes later with a white "Hello my name is" sticker that says "Cherry" stuck to her low-cut black tank.

"Subtle," Jules deadpans.

I turn back toward the stage but end up doing a double take on the way.

Down at the other end of the bar is a man who's so beautiful I nearly swallow my straw. His navy dress shirt is rolled to the elbows and tugs over broad shoulders as he reaches for his drink. Dark hair extends past his jaw. Add that to the straight nose, firm mouth, eyes that scan the room...

Those eyes stop when they meet mine.

It's electric, the connection. I swear he looks into me, through me. Fire grabs my core, making my breasts tighten.

"Liv. You okay?" Jules asks.

I blink, ripping my gaze from his. "Yeah."

I shake off the unsettling attraction.

He's the opposite of my boyfriend, Adam, who's blond and athletic with an easy smile. He's from the right family, has the right hair, and is point guard on the basketball team.

"No fucking way."

Kat's pointing at a booth in the back, where a couple of guys from the basketball team sit, plus one I don't want to recognize.

Adam is sprawled across the bench with a half-naked woman bent over him, her boobs swinging dangerously close to his face.

My throat tightens as I wait for him to push her away.

Instead, he shifts back, grinning, and invites her closer.

"Unbelievable," Kat bites out. "I'm going to fuck him up."

Jules squeezes my shoulder, and I shake her off.

"Don't, Kat. It's probably some basketball team thing."

I turn toward the front, ignoring the back of the room and the burning behind my eyes.

What I didn't tell Kat or Jules to avoid spoiling the birthday vibes is that when I showed up at his house yesterday morning, a girl was slipping out of his room.

Something in my chest popped like the cork on bad champagne.

I told myself if I dated Adam, at least one part of my life would go as planned. After twelve years of wasted ballet, I couldn't be a dancer like my mother, but I had him.

We've invested three years. We'll figure this out. Maybe he screwed up, but he loves me.

I wonder if love feels the same for him as it does for me. If it's that dull reassurance I dig my fingers into when I'm feeling lost or if it's something else entirely.

The MC calls the contestants to the stage to explain the rules. "Each contestant has two minutes to dance, then the crowd will vote. First up is Brandy."

The first girl stands up as they play "Pour Some Sugar on Me."

She gyrates her hips, swinging around the pole, clearly drunk.

The next is a little better but not much.

At one point, a woman in the crowd yells, "Camera!" and security descends on a guy filming from inside his jacket with a phone to drag him out of the club.

It's comforting to know they enforce the "no

videotaping" rule. The idea of dancing here on a dare and a few shots of vodka coming back to haunt you in perpetuity thanks to the internet is horrifying.

"Cherry!" the MC calls after a few minutes.

"That's you, Kat," Jules says, jarring me out of my numbness.

She gets up from the bar but trips. "Whoa. I can't, guys."

"You didn't pre-game that hard," Jules points out.

But Kat holds up a flask inside her bag I haven't seen before.

Shit.

Jules motions to the bartender for a water, but movement catches my eye. In the back, the woman dancing on Adam takes his hand, and he follows her with a shit-eating grin toward a doorway with a beaded curtain.

Bile rises up my throat.

I slept with Adam three months into my senior year of high school, after his parents' party for winter break.

He said he liked that I made him wait.

Apparently, he likes that this woman won't.

I pull out my phone and type out a text.

Liv: I can't do this anymore, Adam. I want to break up.

After I hit send, he glances at his phone, shakes his head as if he's the one who can't believe *me*, and follows the woman through the curtain.

My chest squeezes. I told myself I'd let him off the hook if he convinced me what happened with the blonde was a one-time thing.

But it's not.

That callous dismissal of my text burns more than the jealousy. I've always tried to be the daughter my parents want, the girlfriend Adam needs, and none of it matters.

"'I Love Rock and Roll,'" starts up, its catchy hook emanating from the speakers.

The MC shouts for Cherry one more time.

"Liv?" Kat's peeling off the sticker and holding it out, her eyes imploring. "Do it for me?"

I'm not the girl who takes her clothes off when she's angry.

I'm the one who makes the other person feel comfortable, especially if they're the person who screwed up.

But the crowd's sneering faces blur together, and that cork in my chest is back in place, the contents of the bottle under more pressure than before.

I take the sticker and press it to my sleeveless white D&G tank top tucked into denim shorts.

When I start through the crowd, there's a wave of cheers. Each step is more confident than the last.

On stage, the bright lights are familiar, even if the audience of drunk and leering townies isn't.

The last time I danced for a crowd was years ago. Before...everything.

I catch the eye of the beautiful guy at the bar. He's not leering. He's watching as if I'm the only person in this bar worth looking at.

The awareness is back, a tingling that cuts through my numbness. I'm borrowing from the conviction in his eyes.

I stop in front of the pole, then reach back to wrap my hand around it. My back arches, and cheers go up.

I have what Kat calls "a great rack."

I call it "destroyer of dreams." When I turned sixteen, my boobs came in, and my ballet instructors crossed my name off their lists.

Tonight, no judgmental ballerinas are watching, and no beer bottles trip me up.

I lift my leg behind me in an arabesque. My

fingers grab my stiletto, and I tug it toward the back of my head.

The more the crowd cheers, the deeper I go into the music. Into my own head.

The rhythm is low in my gut, and my feet move without instructions.

The tension feels raw and real and true.

I catch his eye again. His nostrils are flared, his jaw tight. For an instant he sees me, unlike everyone else in my life.

I pop my feet wide and sink into the splits.

It's not until I start to roll out of the pose that the sticky floor registers.

I'm barely up to standing when the woman in the uniform is over to me, grabbing my hand and lifting it high.

"Our winner!" She passes me a check. "We have a tradition. You know what it is."

I don't notice the buckets at the side of the stage until two women dump them over me.

The shock of cold drowns me in a wave that steals my breath.

It's not water. It's vodka.

I'm soaked from my shoulders to my toes. My nipples are hard points through my shirt. The only thing still dry is the check in my fingers, its amount less than the price of my alcohol-drowned outfit.

The shock eats into my power trip from being on stage as I stumble down the steps.

"That was epic, Liv!" Kat bellows when I reach them.

Jules bites her lip. "Are you okay?"

"Totally." My arms fold over my chest and the wet fabric sticking to my skin makes me cringe. "I'm going to the car for a sweater. Happy birthday. *Cherry*."

I pass the check to Kat with a wink. She tries to give it back, but I refuse, pushing through the crowd to the exit.

My white Audi is conspicuous in this parking lot. Most of the rest of the cars are more like the Dodge pickup between my car and the club, though there's a beautiful black Mercedes on my opposite side.

I glance back at the club as I fish the keys from my bag.

That's when a group of guys emerges from the door. Adam's one of them, and another guy pulls out a vape pen as they laugh.

"How was it?" one of the other guys asks.

Plink.

I sink to my knees to follow the keys I've dropped.

It's dark, and I fumble around under the edge

of the car. My eyes burn, a tear escaping down my cheek.

The crunch of gravel behind me makes me freeze. "This the after-party?"

I swipe at my face because crying in front of other people is a sign of weakness. When I turn, my heart stops.

It's the guy from the bar. The beautiful one who watched me.

Up close, I'd peg him at late twenties, maybe thirty. He's tall and broad, dark hair grazing his jaw until he shoves it back impatiently.

"I'm not here to perv on you. I'm heading out." He glances at the pickup truck. "Wanted to make sure you weren't driving drunk."

"I'm getting a change of clothes."

His gaze drops to my chest. My nipples are still sticking through the shirt. "Good call."

He starts toward the hood, probably to round to the driver's side of his truck, but I grab his sleeve.

"Don't leave. That's my boyfriend. Ex-boyfriend," I amend, the word I've never used before echoing in my ears. "If you move your truck, he'll see my car."

The gorgeous man looks between the Dodge and the Audi.

"Just...wait until they finish their vape?" I plead.

He doesn't respond but doesn't move either.

I unlock the car and lean into the back seat, rummaging for my sweatshirt. My fingers sink into the soft fabric of the hoodie.

"What are you doing here?" I ask over my shoulder.

"Came to town for some unfinished business."

He's facing the other way to either give me privacy or stand watch.

I tug the sticky shirt over my head, wadding it into a ball and dropping it on the back seat.

"I meant at a strip club. You don't look like the type to ogle tits and drown your sorrows."

The low rumble of laughter behind me makes my skin tingle. "You don't look like the type to shake your tits to forget your problems."

I pull on the sweatshirt and shift back out of the car, the hood still up around my head. "So what's your excuse?"

I catch sight of my reflection in the passenger mirror—smudged makeup, hair plastered to my head except for a chunk that's gotten pulled out to hang alongside my face. But the man turns back to me before I can even think of trying to fix it. "I hate doing what people expect."

"So you didn't ogle my tits?" It's not like me to tease a stranger. Blame it on the vodka fumes.

"I'm a man who appreciates beautiful things."

The heat in his eyes steals my breath. It's like he's talking about watching fireworks or a once-in-a-lifetime meteor shower.

He does a double take at the logo on my chest.

"Russell U. You're an alum, too?"

Before I can respond, riotous laughter goes up from across the lot.

"Fucking A, Adam!"

"Ignore him," he murmurs. I blink up at the man in front of me, who tugs the hood off my head. "Why'd you want me to watch you dance?"

"What makes you think I did?"

"You wanted everyone to, or you wouldn't have been up there. A woman like you is desired. I think you're tired of the reason people desire you."

There's no reason I should be smiling tonight, but the way this man looks at me, like my life isn't over, has me gulping night air.

"I'm Sawyer." He bends to pick up something from the ground. The sticker from my shirt. "Nice to meet you, Cherry."

"Come on, let's get out of here." A voice carries on the breeze.

Adam and the other guys cut across the lot, and my heart rises up my throat as I scan the lot and notice the RU Basketball bumper sticker on the Jeep in the next row.

If they don't notice my car, they'll still notice me when they head this way.

I duck behind Sawyer. "Quick. Act like you're my boyfriend."

A brow lifts. "You want me to pick a fight with you?"

Despite everything, I laugh. "That's what you think of? No, just—" I grab his jacket collar and drag him down to the ground with me.

I land hard enough the gravel scrapes my knee.

We're crouched between the cars. He's inches away, and my heart skips because of how he's looking at me. Not me on stage. Me in my hoodie, makeup smudged.

"You didn't want me to argue with you," he murmurs, a mocking lilt to his voice. "You wanted me to kiss you."

I'm not sure I was thinking at all when I said it. But heat strokes down my spine at the thought of his mouth on mine.

"You make it sound so sexy," I whisper.

"It is sexy." His throat flexes, and the way he says that word is the hottest thing I've ever heard. "A kiss is a promise. A declaration of intent."

"Most guys think anything less than a blowjob doesn't deserve their attention."

Sawyer shifts closer, his gaze knowing. His lips are an inch from mine. I've never felt this kind of chemistry with anyone, and he's practically a stranger.

His fingers find my hair, and I think he's going to tuck it behind my ear but he doesn't—just strokes the back of his hand down my cheek.

"Do me a favor, Cherry. Don't judge me by that tool."

Before I can respond, he leans in and brushes his mouth over mine.

He's warm and firm, confidence without arrogance, and every slide of his lips is pure fucking finesse.

His fingers find my chin, holding me in place. When he changes the angle, taking me deeper, I can't help but open under him.

The gravel is rough on my bare knees, but his kiss is exquisite. He's exquisite. A soft sound escapes me, but it's lost in his mouth.

When he pulls back, it's all I can do not to say wow.

His breathing is rough, too, those gorgeous eyes dilated in the dark.

"You taste like trouble." A thrill races through me. "I'm going to give you my number."

"You're asking me out?"

The surprise on his face is chased by a grin. "Tonight, you're going to let me know you got home safely."

And what about tomorrow?

But as he takes my phone and types in his contact, I'm relieved. Adam cheated on me, and I'll break up with him in person tomorrow...but this is moving fast.

I survey the parking lot. *They're gone.*

I tuck my phone back into my purse and straighten to test whether my knees still work.

He's up the next second too, tall enough his jaw is eye level on me. He checks his watch. "You have to work early too?"

I can't tell him I'm a college junior, and tomorrow is the first day of classes in my third year.

"Let me guess. You'd rather take a bullet," he murmurs.

"You could say that."

"I know the feeling."

What could he dread? He's gorgeous, confident, charismatic in a doesn't-have-to-try way. If adulting is an art, this man is Rembrandt.

"I hope tomorrow's better than you expect. Don't let anyone drag you down, Cherry." His gaze fixes on my legs, and he bends to brush my knee, loosening the bits of gravel stuck to it.

With a look that's pure heat with a side of regret, he rounds my car, heading for the Mercedes on the far side.

I want to beg him to stay when I realize...

The truck isn't his.

Sawyer could have left anytime without my ex spotting me.

He didn't.

When he peels out of the lot, disappearing in a glimmer of red taillights and New York plates, the next breath I take is cold night air and engine fumes.

Nothing ever tasted so good.

2

———

OLIVIA

2:12 AM

Liv: Got home safe. I'm never getting the vodka out of my hair.

2:17 AM

Unknown: You look good dirty. But if it's bothering you, I could come help you wash it out.

2:21 AM

Liv: What a gentleman. Thanks, but I should be fine as long as I don't stand too close to any bonfires this week ;)

2:24 AM

Unknown: Please don't. It would be a crime to watch tits like yours go up in smoke.

2:27 AM
Liv: Wow. That's the nicest thing anyone's ever said about my tits.

2:30 AM
Unknown: To your face.

2:41 AM
Liv: LOL

2:45 AM
Unknown: I've been called a lot of things, but never a gentleman.

2:51 AM
Liv: Are you one?

2:53 AM
Unknown: Do you want me to be?

3:01 AM
Liv: No. I'm over gentlemen.

3:03 AM
Unknown: Bold statement.

3:07 AM
Liv: You know something...Tonight on stage is

the first time I've felt brave in a long time.

3:15 AM
Liv: Okay, that was my weird disclosure to a virtual stranger. Now it's your turn to tell me something or I'm going to go to sleep feeling like a moron.

3:17 AM
Unknown: Well we can't have that.

3:19 AM
Liv: Are you being sarcastic? Wow, you're REALLY not a gentleman.

3:20 AM
Unknown: Hah, I was thinking.

3:22 AM
Unknown: I've been dreading today all week. I haven't been to this town in years. Me being here is going to cause all kinds of problems. The past should stay in the past.

3:24 AM
Liv: That's impossible. Your past makes you who you are.

3:26 AM

Unknown: Beautiful and wise.

3:28 AM

Liv: More compliments? And here I thought all you liked about me was my tits.

3:28 AM

Unknown: Not even close.

3:30 AM

Liv: Maybe today will be better than you think.

3:31 AM

Unknown: It's already exceeded my wildest expectations.

On the first day of classes, the campus is buzzing.

Sororities are rushing. The frosh will be embraced by upper-year students.

It's an orgy of newness and adventure and acceptance and possibility, and both years, I've loved it.

Except both years, I didn't dump my boyfriend the night before.

"I hope your first day of school is everything you want. Remember, first impressions linger. Say hello to Adam for us."

My mother's voicemail rings in my head as I search my closet for outfits.

I stretch on my toes, feeling for my Givenchy denim miniskirt on the top shelf. It's stuck under something, and when I tug it, a cardboard box falls to the floor. I shove the spilled contents, pink and black fabric and feathers, back inside and replace the box.

After dressing, I fasten my hair up in a simple French twist and straighten the full-carat diamond solitaire around my neck.

My mom is right about one thing. First impressions linger.

I reach for the phone on my desk, resisting the urge to read last night's texts for the millionth time.

Sawyer hadn't put his name in my contacts, and I didn't add it because it felt like a secret between us. Naming him in black and white pixels would make him less mysterious.

He said he had to work today. I hope I see him again because I can't stop thinking about that kiss.

Not that I'm looking to jump out of a three-year relationship and into...whatever it would be with a guy like Sawyer, but I've never experienced that kind of connection I felt with him last night.

On impulse, I tug a couple of pieces of hair out of my twist to frame my face before heading out to the living room.

"You look cute." Jules bursts into our shared apartment on campus in shorts and sneakers.

"Thanks." I grab my soft gray Ted Baker sweater that feels cozy and sophisticated at once from its hook by the door. "You're up early."

"Went for a run. Five miles."

I check my nude lipstick and add some bangles of Kat's. We have an open-door policy for borrowing clothes, instituted when we became roommates.

"Want breakfast?" I ask, grabbing a yogurt from the fridge.

"No thanks. I'm late already and need to shower. You seen Kat?"

We stick our heads in her room, but she's already gone. Her computer sits open to the homepage of Russell University Download. We've all lost hours falling into the rabbit hole of gossip on R.U. DOWN.

When I eat my yogurt, a text from Adam comes through.

Adam: Hey babe. We should talk.

Now he wants to talk?

I shove the phone in my bag without responding.

The Stevenson dorm is newer than the stone and ivy buildings, made for upperclassmen in apartment-style residences with three or four rooms each.

As I take the stairs down and start across campus bound for my first class of the new year, I tug the arms of my sweater up to my elbows.

At the end of August, the campus is in full summer bloom. It's postcard perfect with green hills, manicured pathways lined with flower beds, Greek Row at one end, and the elm forest beyond that separates it from the bad part of town east of campus. The good part of town is west, brushing up against the stone gates like rich people rubbing elbows at a charity event.

I wave to some other classmates as I arrive at the stone lecture hall.

"Did you hear?" asks Madison, one of the handful of girls in my cohort. "Professor Lancaster died last week."

"What?" My fingers tighten on the strap of my bag so hard it hurts. "That's impossible."

She shrugs, her red ponytail sweeping over

one shoulder of her Russell Engineering hoodie. "Just passing along the news. I don't know what happened. There'll probably be some TA to make a cursory statement today, then he'll let us out until they can find a replacement."

He couldn't have been more than sixty. His tough exterior hid someone who genuinely wanted his students to do well.

An arm hooks around my neck, and I look up to see Kat.

"You're coming to my engineering class?" I ask as we head inside the building, the wood floors of the theater-style lecture hall creaking under our feet.

"I don't have class until ten thirty. Need to keep an eye on you given what happened with Douchewad. You're too nice a person to treat him the way he deserves."

"I'm not that nice."

"Liv, you brake for squirrels. And frogs. And a dragonfly that one time—"

"You're exaggerating. Besides, animals deserve kindness."

"Unlike Adam."

I take a slow breath. "We're done. I texted him last night."

Her brows shoot up but I'm grateful for her

company when Adam walks in and claims a seat behind us.

When I chose the same major as my boyfriend, I pictured us at graduation together, our proud parents in adjacent seats in the audience.

This scenario never entered my mind.

Adam's hands find my shoulders, and I resist the urge to shove them away as I turn.

"Babe. I heard you were at Velvet last night." His blue eyes search mine, concerned. "That's not your scene."

"It's not," I reply, "but I *saw* you at Velvet. And you weren't alone."

The rest of the class has gone quiet.

A throat clears behind me. "Welcome to mechanical engineering. We will be creating many things in this class. Drama is not one of them. Check your personal lives at the door."

The voice is masculine and irritated, and from the echo, it's coming from the pit at the front of the hall.

"Jesus," Kat breathes.

I face the front, and my entire body tightens.

The man at the head of the class is tall and broad. His beautifully cut jacket sets him apart from even the upper-crust academics at Russell while his dark jeans and too-long hair say he doesn't give a fuck.

But it's his gaze that pins me to my seat, that has heat crawling through me as recognition flares in Sawyer's eyes.

In the light of day, the man I passed the better part of an evening with is more beautiful than I remember.

I swear he memorizes every inch of the sweater clinging to my breasts, the bangles on my wrists, the hair I spent an extra half an hour washing and styling after its misadventures last night.

"Damn," Kat exhales next to me. My roommate shifts, chewing on her pencil and arching an eyebrow. "Think he fucks students?"

I kick her under the desk.

Sawyer finally breaks our loaded eye contact, turning to the rest of the class.

"My name is Professor Redmond. You've more than likely heard the untimely passing of Professor Lancaster. I will be filling in."

Professors don't "fill in" at our school. They're carefully chosen from mountains of elite applications.

But he continues. "I am the founder of a Manhattan company that develops technology solutions for a range of industries. My undergraduate and master's degrees were here at Russell."

The Sawyer Redmond at the head of the class is definitely the man I met last night. But with me, he was mysterious and playful. This version is cool and condescending.

I check my phone, remembering a meeting I had scheduled with Lancaster this week to discuss our design projects.

It's still in the calendar. Eerie. Untouched.

Yesterday, everything was familiar. Today, nothing is.

Emotions collide in my chest, but none of the biggest ones are about Adam. Instead, I'm sad about Professor Lancaster, elated to see the man I met last night, and horrified to see him *here*.

"Well, that was exhilarating," Kat breathes as class wraps up. "Catch you later to get ready for the Omega party?"

"Sure," I say distractedly as she takes off.

What's etiquette for learning the man you kissed the night before is your new professor?

I can't make eye contact and then leave without talking to him.

So I join a line of students at the front of the room.

Sawyer dismisses the first couple of inquiries fast.

The third person in line is a guy named Royce. He comes from a blue-collar family in town and is here on scholarship.

"Professor Redmond, will you be supervising the Stars Engineering Contest design team?"

"No."

"Professor Lancaster always supervised," Royce presses.

"I'm not him." The words are low, Sawyer's smooth tenor lifting the hairs along my arms.

No, you're not.

When he turns his gaze on me, a spike of awareness stabs through me.

Dark, hooded eyes read my soul, seeming to strip away my clothes, my skin, even my thoughts.

"Yes?"

No.

This is wrong. It's wrong that he's here, that I feel as if I want his protection again, that the thing I want his protection from is the fucked-up reality I walked into this morning.

I've thought about you every damned second since we talked.

"Professor," I start, the word feeling heavy and loaded. "Do you know if there will be a service for Professor Lancaster?"

"You'll have to contact the department."

"Babe?" Adam jerks his head from the doorway.

Sawyer spots Adam, his gaze narrowing.

The girl behind me bumps me hard, and I drop my tote. Sawyer and I bend at the same time to grab it.

His arm brushes my breasts, and I suck in a breath at the jolt of electricity.

"Sawyer..."

"It's Professor Redmond to my students." He stares at my red knees an extra beat, but when his gaze finds mine, it's scorching. "Today and every day."

"Liv, wait up." Adam chases me down halfway across the hill, falling into step with me as I make my way toward the Atrium to grab a coffee before the next class. "About last night..."

I turn to face him, my heart thudding against my ribs. "The part where you went to a private room with a stripper? Or the part where I texted you, and you didn't even acknowledge me?"

He sighs and shifts his bag on his back as if this conversation is the most irritating part of his day.

I always tolerated his moods because I

reasoned he had the same pressures as I did, only more so because he's going to take over his father's company. Now, I think I'm over tolerating it.

"Go ahead," I challenge. "Tell me it was a mistake."

"It wasn't a mistake."

My chest aches, which is stupid. This guy I thought I loved cheated on me, and I still want his approval.

"But I don't think you want to break up," he goes on, "or you would've broken up with me ages ago. Our moms probably have the wedding venue booked."

The wind picks up, tugging at the oak branches. It reminds me of the time I ran away near Halloween when I was nine. I rebelled against the new intensive schedule of dance and dieting my mother prescribed and insisted "she didn't love me, and I didn't love her."

I made it to Central Park. Police officers approached me near dark when the pink sweater in my backpack wasn't enough to keep me warm against the cold.

In the town car on the way home, my mom wouldn't let go of my arm, her grip punishingly tight.

"Love is someone who is required to come

and find you when you're stupid," she had said under her breath. "If you give that person too many reasons, they'll stop coming."

I shake off the memory, shoving the hair out of my face. "We're not getting back together."

Adam exhales. "College is a time to learn who you are. If we don't live a little now, we're never going to get the chance."

"Love isn't about being reckless, Adam. It's about security and knowing someone will be there for you."

I turn my back without waiting for a response.

The day I told my parents I intended to enroll in engineering, they were horrified. My mother made me promise I'd consider transferring to a more "appropriate" major.

But I explained I wanted to be with Adam, which seemed to placate them.

It was mostly true. What I learned around the same time was that I like making things. With my brain, my hands.

When I took science in high school, I was going through a tough time with dance and struggling with my body. Science didn't give a fuck about my arches or my boobs. Though I wasn't valedictorian or even close, it was liberating to immerse myself in a world where my results weren't left to the whims of another person.

This spring when I built a battery to power Kat's laptop after hers broke mid-essay right before finals, I felt as much pride as when I got into ballet school. More, because nothing my body or my mom did could take it away.

After my history elective, I tote the treat I picked up at the Atrium to the engineering department.

"Hey, Betty. Happy first week of class."

The department admin looks up from her work. She must be well into her sixties, but her bright red hair is a curly mop on her head, and her shimmery purple eye shadow makes her kind eyes pop. On a floor occupied entirely of men, she's a shining beacon—literally.

When I pass her the teal cupcake with gold sparkles on top, her eyes dance. "That's sweet of you, hon."

"They had them decorated in RU colors. The whole varsity look made me think of you. Get a look at the football team yet?"

"Oh, I'm keeping a close eye on those boys. The QB thinks he's all that, but it's the new runningback who's got the best chance of making the pros. Mark my words."

"Listen, I wanted to ask if there'll be a service for Professor Lancaster."

She sighs, her usually bright face filling with emotion. "You heard. Awful. No one knew he was sick. We'll notify all students by email."

"Can you..." My throat closes up. "Please make sure I get it? He was a special man."

Betty reaches out to pat my hand, her bracelets jangling. "You'll get it, Livvy."

Satisfied, I start to turn away but catch sight of Royce, the guy from class who approached Professor Redmond this morning.

He stares at the bulletin board, eyes glazed over.

"What's wrong?" I ask.

"If we don't have the Stars contest, I'm fucked, Liv."

Design projects are a chance to build something from the ground up and compete for a national prize that includes money and visibility. We've had a team planned since the spring, though Royce organized it, and I was probably only invited because I was in earshot when he invited Adam.

"You'll have lots more time," I point out. "The project would take a ton of hours, every week all year, with no guarantee of winning."

Royce doesn't look consoled. "You don't need

this, but I do. It wasn't just something to put on my resume. It was going to be my ticket to a job after school. Not all of us have their life scripted for them and paid for."

I ignore the jab.

My problems and Royce's are different. But our new professor dismissed him without even listening.

I can't change that Lancaster's gone. But if I can fix this for Royce, it's something I can do for a person who deserves it.

I return to the desk, and Betty looks up. "Professor Redmond said he's not supervising the design contest. Who else could do it?"

Her lips press together. "Most professors are fully committed for the semester. So good luck getting someone."

When I turn back to tell Royce I'm not giving up, he's already gone.

3

OLIVIA

"Did you see your hottie on R.U. DOWN?" Kat nudges me as we shift into seats at the University Center with our lunch trays. "There's a whole thread devoted to Sawyer Redmond. With pictures."

She holds out her phone and points at one of him walking across campus. "This one's my fave. I posted it myself."

"Kat!" I exclaim.

"What? I had a sighting after psych and had to document it for posterity." She shrugs. "It's like the Nature channel. Hotties in the Wild."

Jules claims the chair next to me, shoving her bright ponytail behind her.

Set amidst the aging stone buildings that house faculties from English to engineering, the

UC is a modern installation. Three stories high with glass from ceiling to floor, its upper levels are home to the central administration while the lower level is food vendors and seating, the bookstore, and student services.

Looking out on the university's main outdoor square and the hill beyond from our seats, it's a great place to people watch and feel as if you're at the very beating heart of campus.

Of course, some students would argue that R.U. DOWN is the heart of campus. But it's only a website. Here, you can practically taste the history, the opportunity, the challenge to take the world and make it your own.

Today's definitely been a challenge, I decide as phone buzzes.

Unknown: You can't call me Sawyer.

My heart kicks. *Why is he texting me after he all but told me to fuck off?*

I hear his voice in my head, but instead of imagining the cold tone from this morning, I picture the warm one from last night as I type out a response.

Liv: You already pointed that out. In front of the entire class.

After I hit send, my pulse accelerates.

I'd never dare talk to a professor like that.

But he's not a professor. At least, he wasn't *my* professor the first time I met him. There must be some rule that says I get more leeway given he's had his tongue in my mouth.

Unknown: You should have told me you were a student.

Liv: Because I should've known the hot guy who saved me was going to be my professor?

Unknown: You let me believe you were older. Since you're a junior, I'm guessing you aren't even twenty-one.

Liv: You didn't have a problem with it last night when you kissed me.

Liv: And complimented my tits.

Liv: And offered to come over and wash my hair.

Hmm. Too much leeway?

There's no answer, which irritates me. The way guys have been acting lately—mostly Adam, but partly Sawyer too—has that champagne cork in my chest ready to pop again.

Liv: I'm pissed too.

Unknown: Why?

Liv: I met a guy who wasn't a dick. It was refreshing.

Dots blink on my screen, then stop. Finally, a new message appears.

Unknown: Tell me the kid in class who called you babe wasn't the ex from last night.

My jaw nearly hits the table. He's giving me shit for daring to call him by his first name, then weighing in on my dating life?

Liv: Why do you care, PROFESSOR?

Unknown: I don't care. But if that's who you spend your time with, it's no wonder meeting a real man does it for you.

Asshole!

"Who's blowing up your phone?" Kat leans

toward me. "If it's Adam, I'm gonna tear him a new one."

"It's not." I shove the phone away under the weight of two all-seeing roommate stares. After the week I've already had, I can't keep one more thing inside. "Can you keep this in the vault?"

Jules turns to make sure no one's looking, and Kat bares her teeth at a group of girls who start to take the table next to us then think better of it.

We do the secret handshake we devised last year after Jules' parents split up and we spent the weekend inhaling popcorn and watching *The Parent Trap* remake. We might not be able to control the world, but knowing your friends have your back is the best comfort there is.

"Professor Redmond," I say, "was at Velvet."

"I knew he looked familiar!" Jules exclaims.

"How did I miss that?" Kat demands.

"You had a prior commitment with vodka. Which reminds me...maybe you should go easy."

She waves a hand. "It's fine."

Jules and I exchange a look, and Kat tugs down the front of her shirt. "I said I'm fine, okay? I want to hear about the hottie."

I stab a piece of salad with my fork. "He came out when I was changing at my car. He didn't know I was a student, and we had a connection."

"Connection like...he smiled at you?" Jules asks, her eyes shining.

"Or connection like you fucked like animals in the back of your car?" Kat drawls.

The idea of Sawyer shoving me down in the back seat and yanking up my shirt, his mouth on my chest and his fingers between my thighs sends heat spiralling through me.

"He kissed me and asked me to tell him I got home safely."

Kat pushes her tray away, its contents forgotten. "That's it, I'm officially calling the first Hoes Over Brews of the semester."

Jules rolls her eyes. "We're in the dining hall. There's no beer here."

"I don't care. This is too juicy to wait."

Hoes Over Brews is what we call our girls' night. Good pints and good advice from friends have gotten us through some dark times during the first two years of college.

"You realize you have what everyone on campus wants," Kat states.

I glance at my meal. "A chicken Caesar salad?"

"A direct line to the hottest guy on campus. One that would make Adam look like a pussy."

Heat traces down my spine at the idea of hooking up with Sawyer.

"He's a professor. That's strictly forbidden."

Kat's eyes glint. "And totally hot. You should bang him."

"You would say that." My roomie has a habit of leaping first, looking...never? But it's impossible to blame her, especially given how she spent most of her childhood.

"He's gorgeous, but it's dangerous," Jules says. "Russell U isn't the kind of place to look the other way."

"It's exactly the kind of place to look the other way," Kat argues. "Besides, Liv's dad is a major donor."

"Which means he wouldn't appreciate hearing about a faculty member giving it to his baby girl," Jules insists.

I hold up a hand. "Leaving parents out of this, what self-respecting woman would fuck their professor?"

Kat props her chin in her palms, blinking with mock innocence. "The kind of woman who gets off on the power dynamic as much as he does."

A shiver of anticipation runs through me.

"Kat, I have enough people telling me what to do in my life."

Besides, any interest Sawyer had in me is gone now that he knows I'm a student. And there's no way I'd sleep with him after the shit he gave me in class and about Adam.

Last night all I saw was the mysterious, intense, reckless side of Sawyer Redmond. Today, I got the stubborn, demanding asshole side.

So why do you still want to text him back and tell him you and Adam are done? That him calling you babe was just Adam being Adam?

"You've dated Adam as long as you've owned a vibrator," Kat responds. "So I'm going to let you in on a bit of secret wisdom as someone who's eaten a lot more...variety. Taking orders in your personal life, like where to go to school or who to date? Not sexy. Taking them in your private life..." She dangles her spoon, batting her eyes and licking its length before Jules grabs it out of her hand. "You might like it."

———

Omega parties are the epitome of Greek life.

Jules and Kat and I spend an hour getting ready before heading over to Greek Row.

I'm still seething over Sawyer's texts. I've read the last one so many times I can see it when I close my eyes.

If that's who you spend your time with, it's no wonder meeting a real man does it for you.

I wish he didn't do it for me, but he does. He says he's setting boundaries, meanwhile he's trying to provoke me.

We're heading up the steps of the frat house when I turn to take a pointed, duck-faced selfie with a throng of partiers visible over my shoulder.

I type out a text and send it along with the picture.

Liv: Just checking that you approve of who I'm spending my time with, Professor.

Adrenaline surges through me as I hit send.

I jump when my phone buzzes in my hand.

It's not him, though. It's my mom.

"Olivia. What on earth did you say to Adam? I hear you had a disagreement."

I swallow the groan. *How did word get back to her this fast?*

"It was more than a disagreement—"

"I don't want to hear it! You know who his parents are."

They own the biggest construction firm on the East Coast. My dad's in finance, and this particular merger of families would make up for the fact I was born with a vagina.

I picture my mother's unlined face, her filled lips. She had me at twenty-five, and now at forty-five, she still blames me for her near-perfect figure being marred.

"I know what happened," she says at last.

"You do?" I didn't expect her compassion, but God, do I want it.

"Engineering is too demanding. It's shifted your priorities. Your father and I agreed to let you pursue this. But we're concerned for your well-being. College is a stressful time, and you're not making good decisions."

The lawn is full of already-drunk partiers, and I brush an invisible piece of lint off my skirt with sober hands.

"I'm worried about Emma," she goes on. "She's barely talked about cheerleading this year, and she's started socializing with some less than appropriate students at school."

My stomach clenches. My amazing sister, a junior in high school, is sensitive and creative. I can't stand the thought of anyone—including my mom—crushing that out of her.

"You should be a better example for her," Mom goes on.

"She's a teenager, she's figuring out who she is."

"The rebellion is not appreciated. You never rebelled like that."

Not in public.

"I'll talk to her when I'm home on the weekend," I say at last. "And I'll talk to Adam, too."

I hang up, frustrated as I stalk through the frat house and into the backyard.

I'm not taking him back, but my mom will lose her shit if she finds out we split without me warming her up to the idea first.

A text appears on my screen.

Unknown: I was wrong.

Liv: So now you approve of the company I keep?

Unknown: No. Wrong when I said you were beautiful *and* wise.

Because a girl with a brain can't go to a frat party?

Unbelievable.

As I shove the phone away, a guy in boxers and a beanie with the frat's logo bearing a tray of shooters steps on my foot as he stumbles past.

Pain shoots up my leg and I suck in a breath, cursing.

My gaze follows to see him set the shots on a floating raft in a kiddie pool.

Adam and some friends are next to the pool, Solo cups in hand. A cheer goes up at the sight of new drinks but I'm only focused on my ex.

I stalk over, my heels sinking into the soft grass. "You told my mom we had a fight?"

He's wearing a Lacoste polo I got him for his birthday in the same blue color as his eyes. He checks me out in that quick way people do when they've been together a while. "My mom wanted to confirm I was going to your parents' for dinner this weekend. I said I wasn't sure the invitation still stood."

I'm about to let it slide when I glance past him to see the blonde who walked out of his room, heading over with two cups.

She doesn't notice me as she grabs the back of his collar, reaching around to pass him the cup. "Fucking love this shirt on you."

No. This is not happening.

I shove him backward, and he grabs for her. Their arms windmill as they land ass-first on the raft in the kiddie pool.

Hollers go up, and as petty as my action was,

it feels good. As if for once, I exerted force on the world and it *responded*.

I spot Royce nursing a beer in the corner with some friends, looking miserable. I know what it feels like to have doubts about your future.

He's bet everything on the Stars contest, working his ass off through the school year and over the summer to be ready.

If he can't compete, the biggest opportunity of his life will be gone before it's even started thanks to circumstances beyond his control.

Not if I can help it.

4

OLIVIA

I head to the engineering building fifteen minutes before Professor Redmond's first class, per the online department schedule.

"Twice in two days." Betty's lined face creases as she smiles.

I lean an elbow on the desk. "I need to get into Professor Lancaster's office. I lent him a couple of books, and I was hoping to get them back."

"It'll have to wait until Professor Redmond is here. He'll have my ass if I let you in. You can wait on the bench outside his office. Actually, I need him to sign these papers saying he won't supervise the design team. Can I trust you with these?"

I flash my best smile and take the papers. I have no intention of letting him sign them.

Last night at the Omega party, I locked myself in the bathroom to research Sawyer Redmond. Turns out he worked with Lancaster, then left the academic world after finishing his Ph.D. When he co-founded his company five years ago, there was speculation he had sold out.

So why is he back?

Not my problem. He might not want to be here, but he has a responsibility to his students.

I'm going to remind him.

I head down the hall and sit on the bench.

The sound of doors clicking closed and the elevator have me looking up every minute. No professor.

I check my phone. He's teaching a class in fifteen minutes. Maybe he won't stop at the office first...

"Sawyer Redmond," a smug voice comments from down the hall.

I sit straight up, my bare thighs pressing against the wooden bench.

"Being dean seems to have made you even more self-impressed."

The man is kind of a creep.

"Careful. Some people might love seeing

your face around here, but I know exactly what you did and why you left your company."

I strain to hear, but then he comes around the corner and pulls up when he sees me.

His gaze is hot and flustered. He scans me from head to toe, my shorts, the black tank top, the Tory Burch flats.

"Olivia," I say at last, realizing we haven't actually met.

"I know."

He unlocks the door, pushing it wide. I'm aware of every inch of his body, broad and strong and oh-so-close. Today he's skipped the jacket, opting for a navy button-down shirt. His hair tickles the collar.

"I'm here to talk about the Stars Engineering Contest," I say to preempt his assumption I'm here to stare at him. Or beg him to kiss me again.

He rounds the desk as I follow him inside, dropping his bag onto the seat. "Don't bother. I'm not an academic with ambitions for knowledge and teaching. I have an agenda."

"Collect shot glasses from America's seediest strip joints?"

Irritation clashes with amusement on his face. "I'm headed to class."

"The winners get funding, mentorship, and

basically a ticket to work anywhere they want," I continue. "We have a team, but we need a faculty supervisor."

I set a folder on the desk between us, but Sawyer rounds to the window without even glancing at the paperwork.

"See those students out on the hill?" he murmurs, and my gaze follows his. "They're eager, impressionable, malleable. The next generation of leaders. Hundreds of researchers across the country would kill for this position. But that's not why I'm here."

I cross to stand next to him, pulling up when his shirt brushes my arm. "Then why *are* you here?"

That scornful mouth is inches from mine. His contempt should turn me off, but it's the opposite. I'm used to people pulling their punches, my mother's thinly veiled disapproval or Adam's banal smiles.

Professor Redmond's restless energy is a dog whistle to some dormant instinct.

"You don't know me, Olivia, but I know you. You have a designer wardrobe. A country club father and a yacht club boyfriend and a need for approval that runs so deep they'd have to cut it out of you."

Anger flares in my chest, singeing my lungs. "That's not true."

"I'll make you a bet. If I can guess what you were doing this morning in one try, you'll get out of my office and stay out."

My attention drops to his watch. I thought it was a Rolex, but it's not. The face is made of rock or stone, a rough surface under glass. It's clearly custom, but the opposite of what's on trend.

It's as if he has money, and he wants it and he hates it at the same time.

"And if you can't guess, then you will supervise the Stars team," I counter.

Surprise flickers across his expression. "Why do you care so much?"

I think of Royce. "It's a huge opportunity for some people. And most of us don't get endless chances."

Before he can respond, a clearing throat in the doorway makes us both turn.

"Miss Barclay." The dean looks me up and down, his gaze lingering. "I hope your parents are well. And Jean and David."

"They are, Dean. I saw them last weekend."

"Very good. We're glad to have you back on campus. We are particularly proud of our female engineering students."

I force a smile.

"I'm sure we'll see more of one another. Stay out of trouble."

The dean's gaze flicks to the other man, lingering. *Does he know what happened?*

Impossible.

Still, I can't breathe until the dean continues down the hall.

"Jean and David?" Professor Redmond asks when the dean is gone.

"Adam's parents."

"Adam is the supposed ex. Do all your exes call you babe?" The judgment bleeds out of his tone.

I don't have any other exes. I'm not about to say it, because he's already looking down his straight nose at me.

"You made it clear you're not interested in getting to know me, *Professor* Redmond. So go ahead and guess what I was doing this morning," I prompt, folding my arms.

His attention drops down my body, a lingering perusal that has the hairs lifting on my neck and arms.

"You woke up in bed with your vaping prince. Made plans to meet your friends to get your nails done."

I cock my head. "Which of those is your guess?"

"Neither."

He grabs me, and I suck in a breath as he turns me to point to the streak of crimson paint along the side of my bicep.

Shit.

"You were...redecorating your dorm room."

"Wrong! We had an engineering orientation week event. We wake up the first years and paint the bell Russell red with them. It's been a tradition for decades."

He arches a brow, dismissive, but triumph surges through me.

"Betty wanted me to bring you these forms confirming you won't be taking over Lancaster's role as team supervisor. Since you lost our bet, you don't need them. You do need this."

I lift the folder with the information on the Stars contest. My hand brushes his arm as I pass it to him.

"You were prepared for this ambush," he mutters.

"Not just tits."

His eyes flash at the reminder of our texts before his attention shifts to the papers. I'm giddy with victory.

"You weren't so grumpy when we texted Sunday night."

His biceps flex under the shirt. Thick, dark lashes twitch as he scans the forms. "You weren't such a brat when you moaned in my mouth."

My head snaps around.

There's no way he said that.

He flips the switch on the shredder beneath the desk and feeds the papers from Betty in.

"I'll meet with your team. If your concept is solid and worth my time, I'll supervise."

"But...Those weren't our terms."

He cocks his head. "The only rules I play by are mine. Take it or leave it."

Definitely not a gentleman.

"What choice do I have?"

"You always have a choice, Olivia. Even when you can't control the rules, you decide whether or not you play the game."

As I head out of the engineering building, I catch sight of the bell painted crimson outside and pull up.

"Son of a..."

The window of Sawyer's office has a perfect view.

"What are you making?" Kat asks at the UC later that day as she nods at my sketch.

"Last year, we decided our Stars submission would focus on one of the biggest problems in applied engineering: tracking control. Let's say you're landing a rocket on Mars," I go on at her blank look. "It needs to land gently to avoid damaging it or anything it lands on."

"This is exactly what keeps me up at night."

I roll my eyes. "There are a lot of applications besides space. Rescue missions. Surgeries. Some of the biggest medical companies are developing instruments to do repeated tasks, or work so fine even the best surgeons in the world don't have the dexterity to do."

There's huge money in this area, which is why Royce is interested in making a name and finding a job.

Still, once we have a supervisor, we have to qualify a prototype. Which means we first have to build one.

After a full day of classes and a quick dinner, I head to the meeting at the Engineering and Design Lab, half a floor with state-of-the-art equipment for robotics, CAD, and machining.

When I arrive, Madison is already getting comfortable.

I check my phone. "Have you seen the guys?"

"Not yet." She shifts back onto a stool. "I know we talked about building a tracking mod last year, but that's going to be way too complicated. I made some revisions. Since I'm going to be the team lead."

"We didn't decide that."

Royce is our coder. Adam's along for the ride, but he's not bad at building. I'm doing hardware and software integration. Madison does design, but apparently, she wants to run the show.

Her gaze narrows. "I'm the only one with leadership experience."

"I'm not saying I have a problem with it, but we need to discuss it as a group."

I don't want to run the show, but I don't want her to run over our ideas either. Royce wants this badly, he'd be the best choice.

The two guys trip in the door together, laughing. They stop when they see us.

"Boys. We decided I was going to be team lead. Help Olivia remember."

Madison was the only other girl who wanted to be on a design team, but now I'm regretting that she's included.

"Trouble in paradise?" Motion by the door has us turning.

Professor Redmond is there. He must be done teaching for the day, and fuck me if he's not walking sex. The sweater pulls across broad shoulders and strong arms, his hair falling across his face.

"Professor," Madison gushes. Apparently, I'm not the only one affected. "We didn't see you."

"Where's the prototype?" He looks from one of us to the next, his attention finally landing on me. "The rules say you need to qualify one in thirty days."

"We were starting tonight," Royce fills in. "But I was working on some code over the summer—"

"Who's the team leader?"

"I am," Madison said, confident.

Madison and I look at each other.

Adam crosses to me, leaning in close enough I'm aware of Sawyer's heavy gaze when Adam murmurs, "Who else is it gonna be, Liv. You?"

Before I can say that's not what I meant, the lab is plunged into darkness.

Madison shrieks, and I jump.

"The fuck?" Adam demands.

"This must be a prank," I say. Or the byproduct of one. Engineers play the most pranks during the first week of school.

A light goes on. Sawyer's phone.

The rest of us follow suit, reaching for our devices, but Madison's already speaking up. "I'll call the campus facilities department and get them over here."

She dials a number and starts to talk but is cut off when she's put on hold.

Our professor is right. We can't waste time. No one notices as I slip to the door and down the hall.

I've spent many hours in this building, and my key card opens the boiler room.

I prop the door open for any extra light from the emergency strips in the halls and pop open the fuse box.

"What are you doing?" Madison's voice makes me stiffen.

"The fuse for the lab is blown. More than one, it looks like."

"Maintenance won't come until morning."

I brush past her for a toolbox.

Footsteps in the hall have the hairs lifting on my neck.

"Professor," Madison says when the footsteps stop nearby. "She's going to burn the place down."

What the hell? It's not like we were best friends, but it seems as if she has it out for me.

"Madison, give us a moment." Professor Redmond's voice is deadly low.

Her footsteps and the light from her phone disappear down the hall.

"What exactly are you doing, Olivia?"

"Trying to get the power back on. I get that we're supposed to wait for the facilities guys, but we don't have time to waste, and—"

"Fix it. And make it fast."

Sawyer's not saying no, like my parents and Adam.

He's saying full steam ahead no matter the consequences.

It's exhilarating.

I turn to the industrial shelving on the far wall, poking through bins in search of a replacement fuse.

The man in my space follows, holding the light. "Do I want to know how you have a key for this room?"

"I rehearse my dance moves in here between amateur nights."

"You are quite talented. You must have attended stripper school." His voice is warm in the dark.

"Of course. I have badges for spins, pole work, and of course I got the highest merit for my vodka absorption skills."

"Really?"

"No. But I did take ballet my entire life."

Nothing in the first bin. I turn to the second.

"You're full of surprises. You also failed to mention your team was in shambles when you recruited me."

Sure, what he walked in on a few minutes ago probably wasn't what he expected.

"I don't know what's up Madison's ass. But since Adam and I broke up—"

"Those words, 'broke up,' don't mean what you think they mean. The common interpretation is that you're no longer spending time together. The nicknames stop. So does the touching."

"Why do you care?" If I didn't know better, I'd think he was jealous. Which is impossible.

"I don't enjoy watching smart girls waste their time chasing useless tools."

"Well, at this moment, I'm only chasing a useful tool." I find the fuse, triumphant, and cross back to the box.

"He was the perfect boyfriend," I hear myself say. "Until he wasn't."

"What changed?"

"He cheated on me." I take his hand and move it to where I want the light. A shiver of awareness runs through me that lingers after I pull my hand back.

"There's no such thing as the perfect

boyfriend, Olivia. But any man who decides you're not enough is severely damaged. He doesn't deserve to look at you."

The fierceness in his voice nearly makes me drop my tools.

"You wouldn't understand," I murmur. "Our families go way back. It's not as simple as me deciding it's over. There are moms and dinners and a whole array of plans that are bigger than either me or Adam."

"Tell them to live their own lives and stay out of yours."

I laugh under my breath as I work. "A lot of people are invested in *your* life, Professor." It sounds like a name when I say it, not a title, and I lick my lips. "There's a whole thread about you on R.U. DOWN."

"Are you what?" he repeats, confusion blurring with irritation in his voice.

"It's a campus website where people post social information, gossip, events, conspiracy theories..."

"Which am I?"

I grin. "All of the above."

He shifts closer, and I get a hit of his scent. Clean, male, dangerous. I force myself to focus when he says, "I told you coming back here would be terrible."

When I realize he's referring to our texts Sunday night, before he turned into an asshole, my chest expands with hope.

"It doesn't have to be. If you don't want undergrads hitting on you, then stop dressing like that. And you should probably cut your hair. Don't frown so much."

"Frowning is what lands me on R.U. DOWN?"

"Just the way your mouth looks when you do." I shake my head to clear it, because I'm dangerously close to flirting again. "Do you know what's happening with Lancaster's house? Like his fish. Has anyone taken care of them?"

"Doubt it."

My hands shake with dismay. "It's important. I'm not talking about goldfish. It's this huge tank with clownfish and—"

"You've been to his house?"

I don't want to get into the details. "That's not the point. Someone needs to check on them."

His light moves to his face, and I'm struck by how handsome he is.

Attraction curls in my stomach, tracing up to my breasts and making my nipples pull tight against my bra.

"If I promise to feed the fish," he drawls, "will it get this fuse fixed faster?"

"Yes." I turn back to the fuse box, relief letting me breathe more easily. "Why do you hate Lancaster? I thought he was your supervisor when you went to school here."

I work away, the silence stretching long enough I think he didn't hear the question.

"Worse," he says at last. "The man was my father."

I turn toward him, bumping against his chest when he's closer than I expect. I lift the light to my face so he can see me.

This whole week, I've been thinking Sawyer Redmond didn't give a shit about anyone, including the man he replaced. But his dad just died and he's been trying to cope with it in the best way he can.

That's why he was dreading this week.

"I'm sorry," I murmur. "God, Sawyer, I'm so fucking sorry."

"Don't call me that." The biting edge is there in his voice, and I ignore it.

We're close in the dark, but I step closer.

When my hands find his arm, he jerks, and my other palm lands on his chest.

He hisses out a breath but doesn't pull back. I can smell him, warm and intense. And he feels amazing beneath my hands.

"Olivia..." he warns.

Before I can overthink it, I press up on my toes and brush my lips across his.

I have no idea what I'm doing except that I need to be close to him, to show him that I'm here for him.

He's hard and delicious, and when the phone clatters to the floor, light extinguishing...

It's us in the dark.

This was a bad idea. I'm regretting my impulsiveness even as I soak in his closeness, his warmth, the feel of his firm lips beneath mine.

Then everything changes.

His breath shudders out. His hands find my sides, sliding down to squeeze my ass as he kisses me back.

My shoulders hit the shelf as he shoves me into it, his lips never leaving mine.

I reach up to grab his silky hair to anchor myself against the attack of his mouth and hands.

I know what I felt in him before, those emotions roiling beneath the surface—grief. Anger.

He looses them all on me.

I've never been touched like this, but it's raw and thrilling. I'm coming unhinged with every sweep of his tongue.

The building might be short on power, but

there's no lack of sparks flowing between us. I'm a live wire in his hands.

Sawyer seeks out my need to be perfect and destroys it.

"Professor?" calls Madison from the hall.

We jump apart, panting.

I twist around and fumble for the breaker. Moments later, everything turns back on.

"Yes! Guys, the power's back!" she calls.

Her voice recedes the other way.

I open my eyes and realize I'm locked in the crosshairs of my professor's warm, dark stare.

My sexy, fantasy-worthy professor I just made out with.

His gaze lingers on my mouth. My chest heaves with shallow breaths.

"After you." Sawyer holds the door, and I move past, my shoulder brushing his arm.

We return to the lab. Neither of us says a word.

"Finally." Royce and Adam look up from their phones where they're playing a game.

Madison folds her arms. "As the team lead, I'm concerned Olivia's poor judgment tonight will interfere with her ability to work on the project."

"You can forget that concern because Olivia is team lead," our professor says evenly.

My jaw drops, but Madison looks almost comically offended.

"But we voted…"

Sawyer shuts her down with a look. "I expect drawings in my email tomorrow morning and a prototype before the weekend."

5

OLIVIA

Unknown: Tell me you got home safely.

The message arrived when our team was wrapping up after midnight, culminating in an email of the drawings to Professor Redmond.

When I'm back in our apartment, Kat's door is shut, and Jules is listening to music in her room.

After brushing my teeth and dropping into bed, I type out failed messages. *I had no idea Lancaster was your father. You must be devastated. I can't imagine what it feels like.*

In the end, none of it feels sufficient. So I summon my nerve and press his contact.

"Olivia," he answers. "What's wrong?"

He sounds restless. Like a caged animal prowling.

"I'm home. But I wanted to finish what I started to say earlier about Lancaster—I mean, your dad." My heart thuds dully in my ears. "I'm glad you told me."

I grab for the curtains of the window over my bed, pulling them back to look out at the dark sky peeking through the ghostly trees.

All night, I've been thinking of the kiss, plus what happened before. I've replayed our interactions through this new lens. How even though he was charismatic that first night, he was dreading the day. How angry he was when I brought up Lancaster in class.

"He was a good person," I say. "I'll miss him, and I can understand why you'd miss him too—"

"We hadn't spoken in years, and he wasn't a good person."

His harsh words shock me.

Before I can respond, he continues. "What was *your* relationship with my father?"

My hand tightens on the phone. "I was his student. He believed in me enough to encourage me to do the Stars contest. But, I can't be team lead."

It would be one thing to let myself down, but I don't want to let the team down. Royce is the smartest of all of us. He's a better option.

"You're my choice. If you don't accept, you can find another team lead and another supervisor."

Which means it's over before it's started.

"That's not fair."

"Of course it's not, Olivia. You walk around without a hair out of place. Get another few buckets of vodka dumped on you and maybe you'll realize the world isn't as tidy as you'd like it to be."

His words get under my skin. "I know the world isn't tidy. Just because I try to be a good daughter and a good girlfriend doesn't mean I'm oblivious."

"Then stop going along with it. How long are you going to let some preppy little shit yank up your skirt and eat your perfect pussy because you think you should?"

My hands fist the duvet. I should tell him to mind his own damn business.

What comes out is, "He doesn't."

Dead air fills the line.

Adam has gone down on me, but it's not a

regular thing. He always made a point of how it was for me, which made me feel like I should enjoy it more than I was, and guilty when I didn't.

After an excruciatingly long pause, Sawyer says, "You're going to hang up and go to sleep. But first, I'm going to tell you something that's not very professorial."

Just one thing?

Every part of this conversation has been over the line.

"You're asking my permission?"

"Yes."

"Fine." I'm dying to hear what he's going to come out with next.

He doesn't disappoint.

"A real man would make you his every meal, Cherry."

Fire streaks between my thighs.

He says it as if he's starving now, and I can't help imagining what it would be like to have my professor find that kind of satisfaction in me. Whether he'd slowly drive me crazy, those dark eyes on my face to absorb every gasp and shudder, or just yank my legs wide and devour everything he found.

"Goodnight," he says, but I grip the phone tighter.

"Wait!" I'm not ready for him to hang up. "Um...You don't look like Lancaster."

"He was my foster father. He took an interest because I was smart. Disruptive, according to any teachers I had, but quick. A lot of kids who caused problems ended up in situations far worse. Everything I earn while I'm in town, I'm donating to support kids in a similar position."

My heart aches for him. "That's decent of you."

"It's not a choice. It's something I have to do."

So he doesn't want to fuck it up.

Like it would if someone found out what we did and he got fired.

"Go to sleep," he says. "It's late. You'll have classes in the morning."

When I clasp the phone to my chest, I'm more awake than before.

***

"We're having a small dinner party Saturday evening. I'll set out the Chanel dress. And your father and I want to talk with you about school."

The short conversation with my mother has me groaning from the time I shift out of bed and stare in the bathroom mirror.

She's going to try to get me to drop engineering and hold next semester's tuition over my head to do it.

I try to pay attention in class, including Sawyer's.

He hasn't cut his hair. Or stopped frowning. He's the object of every girl on campus's fantasy.

As far as I know, I'm the only one he's made out with, and who knows he's Lancaster's kid.

"Human beings are made to invent," Sawyer opens in class. "Stripped of curiosity, we die. But there's a difference between intellectual curiosity and commercial innovation. A gap every person in this room wants to cross, judging by how much you've invested in this education. Who knows the prerequisite to invention?"

"Fat R&D budgets," Royce comments, and a few people laugh.

Sawyer smirks. "Failure. Every success, from the light bulb to the suspension bridge to the moon landing, stands on a grotesque pile of broken dreams, terrible fucking ideas, and ruined reputations."

I shiver a little at the last part.

Madison raises her hand. "Professor, your company has an exceptional track record..."

Why doesn't she drop on her knees and offer to suck him off?

Great. Now I'm jealous.

"...What do you think separates the people who're successful at creating the truly great innovations?"

He doesn't blink. "They're brave enough to risk ending up in the pile."

At the end of class, students line up to swamp him with questions.

He holds up a hand and reaches for his phone. Moments later, a photo comes through by text.

Lancaster's fish feeding.

I smile and text back.

Liv: Now you have to keep feeding them

Unknown: Dammit. You have a bad habit of leaving out pertinent information where I'm concerned.

My laughter echoes off the walls as I head down the hall.

That afternoon, I meet Royce, Adam, and Madison at the lab to work on the deadline our professor gave us.

Madison's still pissed I was made team lead. I don't tell her I'm still thinking about it. Adam seems to sense my distress about the deadline and helps focus the others.

"There's no way we'll have a prototype by the weekend," Madison says.

"Come on. It doesn't need to be a refined model. Just a mounting base and a robotic arm. If we can get it to grip and lift a Pringles container in the air, that's enough."

"You shouldn't have promised Professor Redmond."

I lift my hands in the air. "What did you want me to tell him? It was a condition of him supervising."

"You heard him talk about failure. This could be a lesson. He wants us to implode. If we fail to qualify, he doesn't have to keep supervising the rest of the year."

Okay, so that hadn't occurred to me. I hate the doubt that creeps in, but I shove it away to focus on our work.

I get Madison alone in the hall on the way back from a bathroom break. "What's your problem with me?" I ask. "I don't want there to be competition in our team."

She folds her arms, unmoved. "You might be naïve, but you're not stupid. You can't possibly be oblivious to what happened."

Madison shoves past me, leaving me speechless.

I try to rally the rest of the team. By the end

of the night, we're all fighting, and the machine is no closer to working.

"I'll walk you home," Adam says when we decide to call it for the night.

"Hard pass—"

"Just because we're broken up doesn't mean I'm gonna let you walk across campus alone in the dark."

I wrap my sweater around me against the cold as we brush through the doors.

At this time of night, Russell U is a quiet kind of beautiful. The paths crisscrossing through campus are lit with lantern posts. The library is still open while most of the rest of the buildings are shut and dark.

"I get that you want to win this," he says. "I want to win, too. Basketball isn't gonna be my future even though Coach thinks I could get drafted. My dad would murder me."

"You'd really sacrifice your future for the one they picture for you?"

"Isn't that what you've always done?"

I turn that over as we pick a familiar path down one of the brick laneways that leads from engineering to the other side of campus where I live.

A few steps along, my phone buzzes with a text.

Unknown: Did you finish in the lab for tonight?

Sawyer must have seen it booked out by our team in the schedule.

Liv: Just leaving, Professor. I'd tell you about our progress, but it's top secret.

Unknown: Tell me you're not walking alone.

Liv: Adam's with me.

"Let me guess, you're late for a reality TV binge session with Kat and Jules?" Adam asks.

"Something like that."

There's no immediate response to my text, and I tuck the phone away.

"Come for dinner at my parents' this weekend," I say, thinking of my mom's call. "I don't want to get back together, but I can't tell them about us until after I get the tuition money for next semester."

He frowns. "This is a bad idea."

"You owe me."

His groan fills the night. "Fine. But don't blame me when this blows up in your face, though."

"What do you mean?"

The grin I used to look forward to is patroniz-ing. "Babe. You're out of your depth."

Before I go to sleep, I send off a text.

Liv: I'll do it. I'll supervise the team.

6

———

OLIVIA

"Are they *all* broken?" I ask.

"Still taste good." Royce devours a handful of Pringles pieces shattered during our prototype testing.

We built a platform with a metal arm attached to it, but the gripping part proved harder than we thought, and when the arm swung into the air, it dropped the container. The chips crashed to the ground every time.

Finally, we had a breakthrough and managed to get lucky once—the machine held the container for three long seconds before it fell.

We emailed a clip to Professor Redmond just in time to meet his weekend deadline, and we're now bound for a party with a bag of Pringles containers.

On impulse, I send off a private text—a selfie of our team with the primitive robot. In it, I'm wedged between Madison and Adam, whose arm is locked around my neck to hold us steady as I take the picture. Royce is positioned behind the robot like he's licking it.

Liv: We made a thing. You proud, Professor?

I lower my phone as Adam catches up, popping the lid on one can. "You do the honors."

Somehow, there's one perfect, intact chip on top.

"Oh my God, that's good," I say.

He grins, his gaze flicking over my outfit.

I didn't have time to change before the party, and I'm wearing a black sleeveless top, a black leather skirt, and tennis shoes. My sweater is tossed over the strap of my bag given the hot day, leaving my tank clinging to my body. My hair is still mostly in the knot on my head, but it was falling in my face as we worked.

"You gonna fix that before we get there?" Adam pokes at it with a finger.

I feel the messy bump. "Fuck it. I like it."

I'm still turning over what he agreed to do for me this weekend as we head for the frat house. Things with my parents are far from stable, but

Adam's like their snake charmer. One hit of him and they'll simmer down.

As we reach the frat house, I check my texts. Still no return message from Sawyer.

What's he doing on a Friday afternoon? What about Friday evening?

Just when I'm about to put the phone away, it jumps in my hand.

Unknown: I expected better.

Unknown: But by all means, go celebrate your mediocrity.

My stomach sinks.

He hates our work. *My* work, because I'm the team leader.

What more could we have done in the past week? Sure, there was some friction getting off the ground, but we busted our asses to meet his deadline.

A lump rises up my throat. This entire week, I've been so focused on the attraction between us, I didn't realize how much I wanted to please him, too. Sawyer's move to appoint me team lead gave me the idea I could actually do this. I borrowed his confidence, and hearing him take it back guts me.

"You want to bang him."

I shove my phone in the butt pocket of my skirt halfway up the steps to look at Madison. "We broke up."

"Not Adam. Professor Redmond. I see how you look at him."

I square to face her. "You want me to say he's hot? It's not a crime to notice."

Her gaze narrows. "Everything I have, I've worked for. It must be nice for things to fall into your lap. Of course, it probably helps when you spread your legs."

She leaves me speechless, and it takes a minute for me to head inside to find my roommates.

"What's wrong?" Kat asks when I cross to them, immediately reading my face.

"Madison thinks everything falls into my lap." I take the drink she offers and drain it in one long gulp.

My roommates exchange a look.

"Which is crazy," I press, grabbing another drink from a passing frat pledge with a tray, "because I don't have anything figured out. The only guy I want doesn't want me."

I drink this cup too.

"He's reckless, and dangerous, and when I'm

with him, it's like he's this storm I want to walk into and get carried away."

The idea of it sends shivers through me.

"Liv, I—"

"And the thing is," I interrupt, crumpling the empty cup in my hand, "I've always done what I should. And I don't want to do it anymore."

Even if Sawyer felt the same—which he doesn't, because he just told me I'm not good enough—he'd get fired, and we'd be out of this competition, and my hopes of landing a career in this field would be shot. I'd forever be the girl who slept with her professor to get ahead.

"What's that beeping?" Jules asks.

I hear it too.

It's coming from...

I grab the phone in my pocket, turning up the black screen with the dial pad.

Unknown
Call duration: 54 seconds

No.

I butt-dialed Professor Redmond, literally.

Did he hear me talk about him?

This is humiliating. I've been saying how much I want him, how he affects me, and he feels nothing.

Before I can decide what to do, the lights in the party dim, and an image is projected on the wall.

"Ladies and gentlemen, Omega fraternity presents a mashup for your viewing pleasure."

The first thing I notice in the video is the familiar neon lights.

The second is the classic party anthems, drowned out by the hollers in the background.

When a woman appears in the frame above the crowd, grabbing a pole like a lifeline and grinding on it, my stomach knots.

"Is that...from Velvet?" Jules gasps.

"There wasn't supposed to be a video," I say, numb.

But there is.

One girl, then another.

Finally...me.

I can't look away.

Adam appears at my shoulder with a drink. His gaze lifts to the screen and locks on it. "What the fuck?"

"Shit," Madison breathes behind me. "The second this hits R.U. DOWN, you're over, Olivia. You'll have to leave Russell. Your parents won't let you go anywhere. They'll lock you up until everyone forgets. What will that take, years?"

I pull away, turning on my heel.

"Liv!" Adam calls.

I ignore him and shove out the door, tripping on Solo cups.

My eyes burn as I stalk down Greek Row. I don't know where I'm going, but I need to get out of here.

Instead of turning left to walk across the campus, I continue straight and onto the street north of the school with the big, beautiful houses with stone walls and curved gables.

I stop halfway down and stare up at the façade.

There's no car in the driveway, save Lancaster's. No lights on in the windows.

I round the side of the house to the sprawling, familiar backyard.

It's not like the campus. No eyes to judge me. No expectations.

I yank off my shoes and lie on my back, letting the cool grass thread between my toes.

My life is over.

Okay maybe not actually.

But Olivia Barclay dancing on stage at a seedy strip club on amateur night might as well be a sex tape.

"You'd probably tell me to get over it," I murmur to the sky.

There's no answer. Lancaster, who was a part

of my life in a way no one would understand, is gone.

He never told me he was sick. Never warned me he'd be leaving so abruptly.

The stars shine at me through the gap in the trees on either side of the yard.

I pull up my phone, hoping the video isn't online. But when I open the R.U. DOWN page, it's there. With comments.

SUBJECT: OB dropping like it's hot at Velvet
—Who's OB?
—Olivia Barclay
—Great tits. Needs more ass to balance them out.
—What a slut. I'd pay her to dance.

I tried to do the right thing my entire life. In one week, I managed to fuck it up.

The sound of car doors slamming has me jerking upright.

Someone's here.

Lights go on in the house. I bolt upright, grabbing my shoes, and try to sneak quietly around the driveway to the front.

When I spot the familiar Mercedes sitting in front of Lancaster's, I freeze.

I make it halfway down the driveway, creeping along the asphalt.

When I trip on something, the pain makes me gasp.

The front door cracks, and I hear voices from the house.

I duck low, holding my foot. It doesn't seem to be bleeding, so I set it down and start to make a run for it.

I'm shoved up against the car. The breath leaves my body in a whoosh.

"What are you doing, Olivia?"

Sawyer's here. Not here at the house, but here in my space. He's wearing a dark shirt over jeans, his hair coming loose from where it's tied back. His dark, male scent invades my nostrils.

"Have you been drinking?" he presses.

"I'm not drunk. Maybe this would be better if I was." I laugh. "This is your fault. If you hadn't made me team lead, my ass wouldn't be all over the internet."

In the light of day, I'll probably decide I'm being unreasonable, but this isn't the day.

His jaw tics, his eyes unreadable in shadow. "I have no idea what you're talking about."

"It's easy for you, isn't it? Telling the world to fuck off. Nothing throws you, not your dad dying, not starting a new job, not making an entire campus swoon over you. But me? I'm breaking."

My eyes burn.

"I hate that Lancaster's gone. That he died alone. I hate that there was a side of him that I didn't know. One that hurt you."

I think of Adam.

"I hate that the guy I spent three years of my life with cheated on me, and I hate how much I don't care."

Finally, my attention turns to the man in front of me.

"Mostly, I hate that I met you Sunday night because I let myself believe I was wrong about the world and my imperfect, insignificant self, and you were going to prove it to me."

The first tear slides down my cheek. I start to swipe it away, then stop.

"But it's a lie. You're one more thing I shouldn't want and will never have."

I sneak a hand into his pocket until my fingers close around the object inside. I withdraw the phone and lift the screen before he can stop me.

Call from: Cherry

His eyes darken, a million emotions colliding within them.

I kept him as Unknown in my phone because it preserved the way we met, how mysterious and different he was.

He did the same. I'm Olivia in class, but after hours, I'm still the girl he met at Velvet.

"Sawyer? Is everything okay?" A woman's voice comes from the house.

He shoves me down. His grip on my hair forces my head against his chest, and the car and his body block me from view.

"Be right there," he calls back.

My eyes close as I breathe him in, feel his hard muscles beneath me.

Who's the woman? Was he on a date?

There's a click far away. The front door closing.

"Sawyer," I say.

It's two syllables, but sounds like an entire story, with a beginning and an end and a hundred triumphs and heartbreaks in between.

He drags my head up. He's so close I can see his eyelashes when he blinks.

I lick my dry lips and say it again. "Sawyer. Sawyer—"

"Stop."

"Why? Just because her parents hooked up a

few years before mine, she gets to call you by your name and I don't?"

I hope he hears the attitude and not the hurt beneath it.

"You can regret meeting me, Cherry." His voice is low, like the crunch of gravel under tires. "But I don't regret meeting you."

His thumb strokes my cheek, clinging to my damp skin.

The first brush of his lips is a rough slide of warmth, a hint of wine and comfort.

I inhale that and his scent—dark, masculine. He's a drug I don't want because I know he'll melt my resistance.

But when my lips part to tell him, everything changes.

Sawyer shoves me up against the car. His body crowds me, one hand spanning my stomach.

His tongue tattoos mine.

Deliberate.

Devastating.

I thread my fingers in his hair, but he pins my wrist in a lightning quick move. He grinds against me, his hardness digging into my stom-ach. He's big and thick and so turned on.

I rub my breasts on his chest, needing fric-tion, needing anything.

His hands streak under my skirt, up the insides of my thighs.

It feels so good and I arch to get closer. *More.*

Sawyer's breathing gets rough, and he slips around the fabric panel to press where I'm suddenly wet.

His thick finger probes me until he's all the way in, his knuckles digging into my skin.

My head falls back to hit the car, my eyes unseeing on the sky above us.

Pleasure. Need. Torture. He delivers all of it until I'm gasping, clenching around him.

I'm throbbing, alive, and raw.

The touch of his fingers has me careening off a cliff I never saw approaching, biting my cheek to swallow the sounds of my own pleasure.

After, he pulls back an inch, my rough breath mingling with his in the cool night air. He's braced against the car, panting.

My heart hammers against my ribs and in my ears. My face stings from salty tears.

Sawyer rubs a damp finger along my lower lip. Then his mouth finds mine once more, as if needing to savor every part of me.

"First lesson, Cherry," he rasps against my lips. "Perfect is boring. Trouble tastes sweeter."

If that was the first lesson...

I want the second.

7

SAWYER

It's amazing how many people think a car is a mode of transportation.

The Mercedes I bought three years ago wasn't necessary or even convenient in New York. People who drive cars like mine buy one as a trophy, a rite of passage, or a fuck you to everyone who doubted them from the time they were young.

But as I turn down my former street Saturday morning, my grip tightening on the leather steering wheel, there's no one to receive the universal bird I'm flipping.

My dad's car is at the end by the detached garage. After I park my Mercedes and cut the engine, I stare at the Buick a moment before heading up the stone steps to the front door. It's my third time here this week, and I'm not ready to give up my reservation at the Marriott.

Now, as my feet creak on the faded wooden porch, emotions wash over me that I didn't expect at all.

Anger. Defiance.

Regret.

When I got word he was dead, my first thought was, this is a stunt. He's trying to get my attention.

It worked.

On impulse, I press the doorbell.

There's no echo of chimes, like there was in the years I lived here.

Perhaps like the rest of the house, it fell into disrepair and was never attended to. He took interest in a narrow range of things, and everything else—everyone else—was neglected.

A noise behind me makes me turn, but it's only a car passing on the road. A stranger waves, but I don't wave back.

My gaze fixes to the spot I found Olivia last night.

I'm here with a mission, and she could ruin my chances of accomplishing it before I've even started.

I should've known she'd be trouble the second I saw her dance at Velvet, her body as sinful as her face was sweet. Not to mention when she showed up in my class.

But when she appeared in my driveway, glaring and cursing at me like I'm the devil in her life? Yeah, I pushed back.

I didn't plan on things going as far as they did, but when I touched her, she flew apart in seconds. As if she's been waiting for me.

My phone vibrates with an email from the web host of R.U. DOWN.

Thank you for making us aware, the email reads. ***We are taking steps to remove the content...***

This morning, I tried to make sense of what Olivia said about her ass being on the internet. Didn't take me long to find the video.

Watching it, I was transported back to that night.

But whoever filmed it through the crowd didn't see what I saw. Neither did the students saying heinous shit about her.

So I sent a scathing takedown demand, pointing out how it would bite them to have an under twenty-one student filmed at an adult venue without her consent.

Satisfied, I take a step to one side, reaching for the stuffed mailbox.

My shoe goes through the wood.

I fall, landing on an uneven surface two feet below. "Fucking hell."

"Need help?" A voice calls from behind me.

I glance over my shoulder to find a guy around my age with a strong build and trimmed dark hair, a Heineken in one hand. His jeans are dark and clean, his T-shirt new.

"Well, look who it is."

Daniel extends his free hand to help me up.

My pants are ripped, and it feels as if a hundred splinters have found their way into my thigh.

"You gonna bleed out?" he asks cheerfully.

"One can hope." I probe my leg. The fabric is torn but the skin underneath is only scratched. "What're you doing here?"

"We've been friends since we were kids." He nods to the house across the road with gleaming white woodwork, a wraparound porch, and a round gable on the right side. He glances at the iron ring on my pinkie finger. "You suck at visiting. It's been three years since I accepted a teaching position at Russell. Two since my parents sold me the place."

I bend to inspect the hole in the porch. When I pry the edge of a board with my fingers, it crumbles in my grip.

"You're not helping the reputation," Daniel says.

I brush my hands off and look up at him.

"The street." He gestures along the tree-lined drive. "It's Cypress Lane, but apparently the students call it Hot Profs Lane now. These houses"—he points to at least six—"are all faculty. The school has brought in a lot of younger assistant professors who lucked out finding homes so close to campus."

I have things to accomplish with this house —including, it appears, replacing the porch. The welcome wagon wasn't part of the plan.

But Daniel's the closest thing to a best friend I have.

"You want to come in for a drink?"

He holds up his beer. "You would say that seeing as how I've already got one."

My friend's grin is contagious, and I can't help smiling too.

I unlock the door with the key and step inside.

The floorboards creak under my feet as I cross the threshold.

I don't have far to go. The fish tank is in the living room, blue angelfish and some smaller yellow fish, under the image of the moon landing, across from a faded leather couch and chair.

The television in the corner is tiny—a twelve-inch box that was here when I was.

"Huh. Did not know he was a fish guy," Daniel comments.

"You haven't been over here."

"Nope. He'd say hi when I said it first, but kept to himself for the most part."

I shake my head. "It's remarkable he's invested in any living thing."

A slim, shiny black fish I hadn't noticed before slips out from between some grasses.

"Probably a surrogate for you. That's Sawyer." He points to the fish. "Looks stubborn."

I shake my head and grab the fish food off the coffee table. When I toss some of the flakes in, the fish descend.

I could never decide which part of my upbringing made me hard. Being given up by my parents, or being chosen and raised by a man who only wanted me for my abilities.

There was no love, except doled out as payment for performance. No joy, except in knowledge.

"So how long are you back?" Daniel takes a sip of his beer.

"Not long. I'm here to cover a class and sort out his assets. Had a realtor here to take a look at the place. She thinks there's some fixing up to do before selling."

"I can recommend some tradespeople, if you like."

I nod. "Thanks."

Because I'm here to teach my dad's class, go through his shit, and get out of here.

Low profile. No attachments.

Olivia would more than interfere with that.

She could blow it up entirely.

I lift my phone and snap a picture of the fish eating. Because she probably wants another update.

Her trusting eyes flash in my mind. She tries so hard to be good for other people. The way she ambushed me at Lancaster's office, unwilling to leave until I agreed to supervise their project...

I should have said no.

But I wanted to show her that the assholes she's pandering to aren't worth it. Life is a never-ending string of places to invest your time and energy, and she's standing in the wrong line.

"How's your kid?" I ask, reminding myself Daniel's here.

"He's doing okay. School was rough, but he's working things out. I'm trying to find him some new hobbies."

"I'm sorry. About your wife."

Daniel's grin fades. "Me too. It was good of you to—you know. What you did."

"Don't mention it."

He looks around, as if hoping she'll appear from some dusty corner.

"I know what it's like to leave things unsaid," he goes on. "This place is a new start for me and Andy. Maybe it will be for you, too." He lifts his beer in a toast. "To new beginnings."

I clink the tin of fish food against his bottle.

New beginnings are a lie. But for now, it feels good to pretend.

8

OLIVIA

My fingers are wet.

Not damp, but genuinely wet. Possibly dripping on the expensive dining room area rug.

Dammit, Kismet.

A light "thwap" sound comes from under the table, and I clear my throat to cover it up.

"Everything all right?" my mother asks.

"Great." I plaster on a smile and wipe my hand on my napkin before settling it into my lap.

The dog noses my palm, demanding more table scraps with prim authority. As if she always lived in the eight-figure townhouse, and never on the streets.

As much as coming home has its downsides, seeing the poodle mix I found and named and begged my parents to keep is one of the best parts.

"Sounds like you've been dabbling in some new ventures," my father says to Adam.

Adam sets his wine on the table fast enough it clinks his plate.

Is he picturing the blonde or the stripper?

"Your father tells us they're purchasing another firm," Dad continues, steepling his hands on the table and ignoring the plate of salmon in front of him.

Relief crosses Adam's features. "They're calling it a merger, because most of the engineers will keep their jobs. But there are no questions as to who's calling the shots."

Our townhouse has designer textiles and rare art. The first time I came home from school, seeing it with fresh eyes, it was almost as if its occupants wanted you to forget there were people living here.

But all I have to do is survive tonight without calamity.

My parents sit at each end of the table. Another couple, clients of my dad's firm, sit on my side, my sister Emma and the clients' their two children opposite. One is a boy Emma's age. Another, a girl the same age as me.

"Dad," I murmur, leaning toward the head of

the table as the other guests strike up a conversation about their Labor Day party in the Hamptons. "Can you send me the money for my tuition and fees for the winter? There's a discount on residence when it's paid in full early," I remind him.

"We'll discuss it after."

I glance at Adam, my evidence of how well I'm playing the part I set out to for my parents' sake, at least until I can figure out how to tell them we split and the future my mother pictured for me isn't going to happen.

"Olivia." It's the daughter, Mari. "You go to Russell U, right? Your name is everywhere since yesterday."

"Why is that?" my father asks, leaning in.

Mari squirms, realizing everyone's listening.

No. No, no no.

Her younger sibling speaks up first. "That's the girl dancing in the video you couldn't stop watching."

"What video?" My mother's voice rises.

Emma's gaze drops beneath the table and it takes a moment for me to realize what she's doing.

"The strip club?!" she blurts before I can stop her.

Everyone falls silent.

After the dishes are cleared, my parents' guests make their excuses.

"What the hell happened?" Emma demands in the hall as our parents say goodbye to their guests and Adam paces the living room. "You don't do crazy things. You're the golden child. Did you lose a bet?"

"It was my roommate's birthday. I had a lapse."

Kismet leans against my legs, reminding me her dinner scraps were hardly sufficient compensation for spending the last two weeks away from her.

Emma lifts her phone to watch the video again, and I swipe it out of her hand. "Come on, enough."

She groans in protest.

I'll always see my kid sister when I look at her—the one who was terrified by thunderstorms, who colored her first white dress green with markers and insisted on keeping invisible friends until she was in the eighth grade.

I went to the summer camps and debutante balls my mom wanted me to so Emma could opt out if she wanted.

I wanted her to be free.

I still do.

"You must have more exciting things to think about than your sister's weekend plans."

"You mean her second dance career?"

I swat at her arm and she yelps, ducking away with a grin.

Kismet lets out a tiny bark at being left out of the game.

"There's this guy," Emma starts, scratching the dog behind her ears. "He has a bike, Liv. Like, a motorcycle. It's hard to compare to a guy who's rough and looks at you like he might kiss you or kill you. Have you ever felt that?"

Emma glances at Adam, biting her cheek. "Of course you haven't."

But her dreamy smile has me remembering the guy I shouldn't be thinking of either.

The front door clicks shut and my parents appear in the hall, looking livid.

"My office. Now."

Kismet ducks her head and whines at the sound of my dad's voice. She starts to follow me into the office, but he shuts the door leaving only a crack of light. Even my dog doesn't dare push her luck.

There's nothing more heinous than watching as my parents inspect a video of me dancing. I shift on my feet, waiting for the explosion.

"What the hell were you thinking?" my dad

bites out when he shoves the phone away. My mother keeps watching, horrified.

"We've given you everything and you waste what gifts you have," my mother says.

I bristle. "I didn't waste anything. It was one mistake and—"

"This isn't even our biggest problem. The firm is facing setbacks." My father shifts in his seat. "Some major tech investments failed to come to fruition."

It's not so much my father's words as the pained way he says them that makes the floor slip out from under me.

"So what does that mean?"

"We're postponing our Aspen holiday. And the renovations we planned for the townhouse are on hold."

"Are we broke?"

"Goodness, no," Mom whispers tightly, her fingers digging into my dad's shoulder.

My chest twists. "Okay, so what's the problem?"

"You're a grown woman, and you can't rely on your father forever."

"That's why I'm in school. When I'm finished, I'll get a job—probably a good one, and—"

"Making enough to rent some studio apartment is no way to live." My mother's gasp fills the room. "You need to think seriously about a situation that will provide for you and your family. You have parents who've done everything for you, a sister who still needs you. That boy"—she lowers her voice and jerks her chin toward the door—"is the answer to everything you want and deserve. You've been building toward this for years. And now you've gone and ruined..."

The door swings wide and she trails off.

"It wasn't her fault. I put her up to it." Adam crosses the carpet and wraps an arm around my shoulders. "It was an irresponsible prank and I'm sorry."

I stare at him. He's laying it on thick and they're buying it.

Did he overhear what my dad was saying? No, for all Adam's flaws and indiscretions, listening at a door isn't him.

But a week ago I didn't think sleeping with strippers was, either.

So what's his angle?

My father smiles faintly. "Olivia, we'll table this conversation for tonight."

When I walk Adam to the front door to say good night, I grab his arm before he can leave. "What was that about?"

He turns on the step. "You danced because of me. Because you were jealous." He scans my body, lingering. "I wish you'd gotten jealous sooner."

Before I can stop him, he brushes his lips across my cheek and shifts into the waiting town car.

9

———

OLIVIA

onday morning, I join Jules for a quick run. We go down Hot Profs Lane, and I tense as we pass Lancaster's house.

There's no sign of Sawyer's Mercedes. It makes me feel as if I imagined Friday night altogether.

"I forgot to tell you. An alum donated a chocolate fountain," Jules calls after I shower and finish getting dressed, heading out into our living room.

"For the dance?"

"Yup."

My roommates and I have served on the committee for Fall Ball, an annual campus charity social and fundraiser, each of the last two years. Tickets are taken care of and the event is happening in less than a week, which means coordinating the last of the decorations and auction items.

"His classmate gave an ice sculpture, and he didn't want to be outdone," Kat declares from the kitchen.

The oven door creaks, and I crane my neck. "Wait—you're baking something before nine in the morning?"

"Is there pot in it?" Jules calls.

"New project." Kat sets a cookie sheet on the stovetop, gesturing proudly to the form standing straight and tall in the middle.

The terracotta colored "project" has a wide base, a slightly narrower column and a flared tip. I'm astounded the entire thing didn't topple in the oven.

"Wow." My brows shoot up. "That's not..."

"...a sex toy?" Jules finishes.

"A handmade, non-toxic, one of a kind sex toy." Kat beams. "It's made out of clay and the glaze is non-absorbent."

"It looks a little...optimistic." The thing is the size of a prizewinning zucchini. "Do you need to sign a waiver to use it?"

"No waiver. And you'll thank me."

Before I can tell Kat there's no way I'm

sticking that inside me, Jules leans closer. "Is it dishwasher safe?"

"Trust me. This will be your new best friend. You'll want to handwash it. I'm sure you want to try it, but it needs to cool off first."

"Of course," I say, solemn.

"How was your weekend at home? Did your parents disown you?"

"Almost." I explain what Adam did.

"Huh. He's still an asshole." Kat checks her phone. "But the video's been taken down."

"Seriously?"

I check over her shoulder and sure enough, the entire thread's been deleted.

Did Adam do that?

It's a bright spot in a messed-up few days.

But as I head to class, I realize the video wasn't taken down soon enough.

Making my way across the hill to my lecture hall, I feel eyes on me, and see small groups of students turn inward when I approach.

Inside my building, things get worse. I ignore the snickers and whistles as I enter the lecture hall. A few shouts of "encore" follow me, including from a group of guys by the door.

A few rows back, Adam waves, slinging his arm over an empty seat next to him.

I pretend not to notice and drop into a seat in the front row instead.

I'm unpacking my books when the TA walks in instead of Sawyer.

"Professor Redmond had another commitment today," the grad student confirms.

I swallow the disappointment.

It's not healthy to be this obsessed with a man, especially one who's got secrets and his own agenda and possibly even a girlfriend.

Even if it's impossible to shove him from my mind altogether, I've got discipline. I'll focus on other things.

I start a list on a sheet of paper.

How to be a badass:

1. Date who I want. (And not who I don't.)

2. Pursue my own career and personal interests.

3. Become financially independent.

That one might be a stretch right now, but it's top of mind since the weekend.

Growing up, I fantasized about freedom but rarely considered the flip side of it—needing to take care of everything for myself.

When I pull up my phone to browse through local job listings, I know exactly how to start.

After finishing classes for the day, I dig out long-unused slippers, tights, and a leotard from my closet before heading to the studio in town.

I'm not sure of the parking situation, so I take the bus rather than my car into Elmwood.

The sign for TwinkleToes graces a three-storey Victorian house. But when I head inside, it's completely refreshed.

The walls are clean and white, the trim a blue so warm and dark it's nearly black.

An elegant, slender woman with sharp eyes and chestnut hair looks up from a desk in an office off the hall.

"Hi. I'm Olivia. I'm here about the posting for a dance teacher."

"Did you apply on JobsApp? HireBunny?"

I shake my head, a sinking feeling in my stomach until she says, "Good. I have no idea how to manage all those computer postings." My lips twitch as she rises and holds out a hand. "I'm Theresa. And I remember you from Velvet."

"Was everyone there?" I ask as I shake her hand.

"I own it."

She follows me out into the hall, where empty coathooks line one wall beneath the stairs. "Changerooms are at the end. The other studio is upstairs," she says.

Part of the other wall has been replaced by windows, and beyond, a dozen girls are practicing.

"I hope this isn't your recruitment."

She laughs. "No. We have two studios, and they're all full with classes until ten at night. You ever teach dance?"

"Not really. But I took it for a long time."

"I could tell from your performance." She's not judging, just stating a fact, and she's the first person in a while who doesn't seem to think I've fucked my life by a sixty-second dance. "I opened this studio two years ago and it's expanding. I'm run off my feet here during the day and at the club at night."

"Can I ask what the pay is?"

Theresa tells me, and I cringe inwardly. I've only ever worked for my dad's company in the summer, and I'm pretty sure they paid me way more than most interns make because this amount doesn't sound like very much.

She checks her watch. "We have a new batch of guppies coming in at four. Why don't you give it a whirl?"

"Guppies?"

"Six- and seven-year-olds."

I shove the pay from my mind and focus on the opportunity. "I'd love to."

Ten minutes later I've been to the pristine changeroom and emerged in a black leotard. Children are funneling in the front door.

They're cute. Girls in tights with hair bows.

A little boy with dark, shaggy hair and serious eyes bumps into me.

"What's your name?"

"Andy."

"Hey, Andy. I'm—"

"This is Miss O," Theresa informs him.

I sound like a dominatrix. I bite my cheek. "Nice to meet you."

Hands appear on the boy's shoulders to steer him toward the room.

Familiar hands, with an iron ring on one finger.

I force my attention up dark jeans, a sweater that clings to every muscle and plane.

"Hello, Miss O."

If Sawyer's as surprised as I am, he's doing a good job covering it up.

"Parents wait here, or outside." Theresa ushers me and the kids toward the studio.

The entire time I'm teaching, I'm freaking out. Does Sawyer have a kid?

I feel his gaze on me through the glass but force myself to focus on the class itself.

It's more an exercise in babysitting but when I can tell they're getting bored, I have them turn toward one another and do pirouettes. Andy's the only boy.

"Boys don't do barrettes," one of the girls says, and Andy frowns.

I feel for him—the rejection, the frustration.

"Boys absolutely do *pirouettes*." I think of turns in second position, which require more core strength than most women have.

By the time we're done, the kids spill back out, some tired, some hyper.

Andy looks around for a moment before Sawyer waves to him.

He doesn't look like Sawyer. But then, Sawyer didn't look like his dad. Maybe Andy's adopted—

"Miss O?" Theresa's voice has me turning back. She smiles. "You're hired. We'll work out the scheduling later."

"Thanks."

"Let me drive you home," Sawyer says when I approach.

We haven't spoken since he made me shatter into a million pieces with his hands and mouth. Every part of me tenses, but I want to know the truth. He accused me of keeping secrets, but he's the expert.

"If I can change first, I'll take the ride, but I can walk from your place." Lancaster's house is only a few blocks from where I live.

He nods and I trade the leotard for my street clothes, leaving my hair in the prim bun.

We get into the car, Sawyer fixing a car seat I didn't notice before we get going.

Andy talks happily in the back. "Miss O, you're my favorite teacher."

Despite the tension, I can't resist smiling in the rear-view mirror. "Thanks, Andy."

"And you're pretty. Isn't she pretty?"

Sawyer glances over. "She's very pretty."

Warmth spreads through my chest and I clear my throat. "Is he...?"

"My neighbor Daniel's son," Sawyer explains.

Relief floods me. "He's why you took the day off."

"Daniel had an emergency and asked me to watch him."

The streets pass, and I soak up the glint of

afternoon sun and the scent of leather beneath me and the man at my side.

Andy starts to sing to himself about a baby shark.

I lower my voice. "Do you want kids?"

"Never."

"I do."

"You're barely old enough to have them."

"That's not true. I'm old enough for a lot of things."

Sawyer's grip on the wheel tightens as we pull into the driveway at his house. By the time we get Andy out of the car, a tall man with straight dark hair and a broad grin is crossing to us from the house across the street.

"Hi, little man."

"Daddy!" Andy throws his arms around the man, who boosts him up.

"Everything good?" Sawyer asks.

"It will be. Thanks again. Hi, I'm Daniel." He holds out a hand, and I realize this could get awkward.

"Liv."

"Miss O taught us to make barrettes today," Andy informs his father.

"Pirouettes," I mouth, and Daniel grins.

"Ah, you're the dance teacher. This is good. After last week he wasn't sure he wanted to go back." Daniel turns to Sawyer. "You both need to come over for a beer. I'll get Andy's dinner fixed. Yeah?"

"Fine," Sawyer agrees first.

I'm still surprised.

"What do you do, Daniel?" I ask as we head through his gorgeous house, a Queen Anne style like most of the ones on this street.

"I'm a professor at Russell."

I cut a look at Sawyer. "A professor."

"How about you?" Daniel asks me.

"I'm in engineering, like your friend." It's strictly true.

"Beautiful and intelligent. I don't know how you get the luck."

"It's not—" I start, but Sawyer cuts me off.

"Me neither."

He strokes a finger down my arm.

No way.

He wants to pretend we're together?

It's confusing, and thrilling. Some kind of game, or perhaps a test.

When Daniel excuses himself to help Andy, I lower my voice. "What are we doing? He's a professor."

"He's my oldest friend."

That sets me back in a different way.

Daniel returns, and Sawyer's gaze narrows with suspicion at my slow smile.

"So Sawyer tells me you two go back," I start.

"Yeah, we grew up together. I lived across town, but stayed for undergrad too. Just moved back recently."

"What was he like in school?"

Sawyer stiffens next to me, but Daniel jumps on the game with a grin. "This guy was crazy. Reckless. He'd jump off the highest diving board at the pool before he even knew how to swim."

Reckless.

It feels like the right word for him, but it's dangerous at the same time.

"Have you decided what you're doing about your dad?" Daniel asks.

"The department notified his colleagues, and most of them want to fly in for it." A grimace. "He's being cremated, which means we can delay the service a few weeks."

We finish our drink and thank Daniel before heading out again.

"Have you fed the fish since the first time?" I ask as I start down the porch, Sawyer leading the way.

"Yeah. After the first one turned belly-up, I figured I should do the others."

I'm already sucking in a breath when he smirks. "It was a joke. You want to see them?"

"No." In the middle of the street, I pull up. "Do you have a girlfriend?"

Sawyer follows my gaze to the spot by the car where he touched me Friday. "You're jealous."

"I'm not jealous. I don't like cheaters. Plus, I want to know where your fingers were before they were on me."

"*In* you," he corrects.

Why is that so much hotter?

"Whatever."

"She's my realtor."

I hate how relieved I am, but knowing he didn't walk away from me and into another woman's arms lifts a weight I didn't realize I was carrying around.

"I trust your ass is off the internet." His change of topic is so smooth I almost miss it.

"How did you..."

"I had it taken down."

My chest expands until it feels as if it might burst.

He did that for me.

Not because he's my professor. Because whether he'll admit it or not, he cared. Like he cared about his friend enough to watch his son and take a day off to do it.

"I should be getting home." I shoulder my bag, full of textbooks and lab reports.

He grabs my wrist. "That's it. No 'thank you, Professor'."

"You did a single nice thing. They don't give medals for human decency."

My answer angers him more. "If I'm such a cretin, why did you get a ride back with me?"

"Why did you pretend we were together in front of Daniel?"

A car comes down the street, and Sawyer uses his hold to tug me to the side of the road.

"You won't tell me, then I'll tell you," I say as the vehicle passes. "It's because you *are* reckless. You give me shit for wanting to be perfect, as if you have a monopoly on empowered living. But you're not free, and you're not happy. So stop telling me how to live my life as if you have all the answers."

His attention drops to my throat. "I wanted to know what it would feel like if you were mine."

My heart kicks in my chest as emotions collide inside of me. Gratitude and longing, regret and frustration.

He wanted to spend time with me. In a strange way, having his friend there made it safe —safe because we couldn't do anything, and because Sawyer trusts Daniel.

But Sawyer's grieving, and I can't afford to be caught up in whatever game he's playing. He's beautiful and dangerous and fucked up, and the most I'll have of him is a few stolen touches in a driveway that leave me wanting more.

The bag on my shoulder is heavier than it was moments ago.

"It would feel like make-believe, because I can't do this. And *you*?" I think of what would happen if a professor was caught with his student. "You *really* can't do this. And we…" I take a breath that does little to steady me.

We just fucking can't.

I'm used to self-discipline, to denying immediate pleasure for eventual satisfaction. But I can't remember wanting something as much as I want to lose myself in his tormented eyes.

"What if I don't accept that?"

"If you don't accept that," I say as I pry his fingers off my arm one at a time, "then you're not as smart as I thought you were, *Professor*."

His gaze burns my back all the way to the end of the block.

10

OLIVIA

When I get to calculus Tuesday, Adam is waiting by the entrance to class.

"Hey." He holds the door, his gaze flicking over my outfit.

"Hi."

A guy in the second row, Remi, holds up his phone and follows my steps across the room.

"Dude, what are you doing?" Adam demands.

Remi lowers the phone with a grin. "Figured there might be another dance. Didn't want to miss this one."

Adam snatches the phone from his hand and throws it on the floor.

Remi protests as he lunges after it, uttering a string of curses. I walk past him and claim a seat in the first row.

"People are still giving you shit for that?" Adam asks under his breath.

"It won't go on forever. The video's down at least."

I start to set my books on the empty seat next to me but Adam drops into the spot first.

He did save my ass this weekend.

"Thanks for covering for me with my parents," I say. "You didn't have to do that."

"I wanted to. How's Fall Ball prep going?" He pulls out his notebook. "Let me guess, Jules is adding artistic flair and Kat's bossing everyone around."

My lips twitch. "Pretty much. Jules and Kat are picking up the slack because I've been preoccupied with this project."

Professor Redmond responded to our team email with comments, saying what we sent him was a start but needs to be more advanced. He sent a massive list of articles for us to read.

It's more encouraging than his "I expected better" text last week, but it reminds me we have a long way to go.

"I ordered two new books from the bookstore." I nod to my bag with a yawn. "Plus, I was up until three watching robotics videos and reading articles on my computer. I see lab results every time I close my eyes."

"Anything I can do to help?" Adam leans in. "I want to win, too. Basketball isn't gonna be my future, no matter how much I'd like it to be. And, for what it's worth, there would still be a job for you at my dad's company once it's mine."

I dig out a blue pen from my bag, plus the pink one I use for figures and underlining. "Thanks."

"When you started in engineering, I figured it was about me. Or to prove something to your parents."

"Maybe it was," I admit.

"But it changed."

"I'd rather bust my ass learning something for me than for someone else, or because I think I should."

He frowns. "Back in high school, we used to talk about our dreams. But you've been distant all year."

I glance up at him in surprise. "That's not true. You stayed over at least two nights a week."

"You were there, but you weren't *there*. You ever think maybe that's why I pulled away in the first place?"

Our calculus professor walks in, and I'm grateful for the excuse to turn toward the front.

"How does it work? If we win this competition," I ask Royce.

I'd emailed him to see if he would meet me privately in the lab that afternoon.

Adam's comments stuck with me long after class. Maybe I was distant with him. But it doesn't make up for how he acted, and the fact that for the first time, I want to do something for *me*.

"Winning? Hah. We'll do well to get through Redmond's Everest-sized pile of articles."

"I read half of them last night. Though the dynamic systems model one was a little over my head."

Royce cocks his head, impressed. "I'll get to that one tonight and we can talk about it."

Except for the email to our entire team, I haven't heard from our professor for the last twenty-four hours.

It's unfair given how I left things between us, but I miss his texts. The black and white pixels made me feel connected to him, as if he was there even when I wasn't looking.

When I finally tried to go to sleep, I found myself thinking of Lancaster's fish tank, the incredible ecosystem he filled it with.

On impulse, I typed out a message.

Liv: You better still be finding time around assigning all those articles to read to feed the fish.

It wasn't crossing a line.

I'm interested in ensuring Lancaster's expensive, beautiful fish survive.

My professor is taking care of them.

At lunch today, I got a picture of the tank with a piece of paper stuck to the outside of the glass: the front page of the newspaper with today's date and headline, kidnapper style.

I laughed until my face hurt.

"First off," Royce continues, bringing me back, "winning is unlikely. There are more than a hundred teams, and we have to qualify."

I fold my arms. "But once we qualify."

"If we qualify," he goes on, grinning, "the top three teams—judged by a panel of industry sponsors—get access to two hundred grand each, and the number one team gets a million to invest in R&D, salaries, whatever they want as long as they progress their idea."

"Wow."

"But first we have to get through regionals—a weekend in New York with a ton of competition. We have to demo a functioning prototype and be in the top half of the field."

Okay, so it won't be easy. What else is new?

I might not immediately grasp advanced topics like Royce does, but I know what it means to push myself every day to do things I didn't know were possible. Dance taught me that much.

"Do you think what we're building is enough to win?"

Royce rubs a hand over his neck. "I don't know. The winning projects tend to have lots of applications."

I circle our project, inspecting the single two-jointed arm hanging off the platform. It looks like...a student project.

"Redmond's right. This isn't there," Royce emphasizes.

"Yet," I correct, determined. "It's not there yet."

"What are you guys looking at?" I ask Kat and Jules Wednesday morning when I leave the shower, still wrapped in a fluffy towel.

They spring apart.

"Just boys being assholes," Kat insists.

But I hold out a hand, and she eventually turns the phone around.

On the screen is a video of a dancer working a pole, dipping and grinding and showing her seriously impressive body in a string bikini and barely-there bra, her nipples sticking through the net mesh.

Except my face is crudely pasted over hers.

"This is on R.U. DOWN?"

"No. But there's a link to it there."

Enough.

I bypass my usual choice of clothing and grab a short, pleated skirt and shirt that leaves two inches of skin around my waist bare.

I rummage through my makeup drawer and grab a deep plum lipstick I bought for an event last year, then slick it on.

Instead of pinning up my hair, I leave it straight. The soft curtain tickles my ears and neck as it swings around my face and slides over my shoulders.

Getting ready takes long enough I don't have

time for breakfast. So, I shove a red apple in my bag on my way out the door.

When I walk into class at eight twenty-eight, every set of eyes is on me.

Adam straightens in his seat on the far side of the room.

Remi, in the front row nearer to the door, reaches out to grab my thigh.

"Fuck, baby, bring that ass on over here."

I pull up and square to face him. "Because it's okay to comment on a girl's body whenever you want, right? That's why we're here, for guys to pass judgment."

Surprise crosses his expression. He recovers with a slow grin. "My dick likes you fine. You'd grind on it like the slut you are."

He's disgusting, and the girl my parents raised is horrified.

But there's a part of me deep down, a stubborn spark that wants to fight rather than run.

I drop my attention to his belt. "Women do that out of necessity, Remi, not pleasure. Your dick's probably too small to feel otherwise."

The classroom explodes with gasps and laughter, and Remi's face turns purple.

"Mr. Attwood." Sawyer's voice has the hairs lifting on my neck. "Eyes front and reattach your jaw. If a woman wants your attention, she'll let you know."

Another round of hollers go up.

I turn to see our professor setting his bag on the desk at the front.

It's only been two days since I've seen Sawyer, and I feel starved for the sight of him. He's wearing dark pants and a pale blue shirt, and he hasn't shaved. As if he's been busy, or distracted.

"Miss Barclay...sit down."

First, he had that video removed. Now, he tries to rescue me in class.

It feels personal.

Instead of being grateful, I'm annoyed.

Remi might be an asshole, but I don't need Professor Redmond saving me, either.

I take one of the only free seats at the far side of the room.

He talks us through stress analysis of mechanical components. He knows his stuff, but seems extra irritable.

Welcome to the club.

I press so hard taking notes that my pen rips through the paper.

"Friday morning is a quiz," he informs us with fifteen minutes remaining in class, and my hand shoots up.

"Friday is Fall Ball," I say. "Professors let students out."

He cocks his head. "The dance is in the morning?"

"No, but I'm on the events committee for student council, plus Engineering Society is sponsoring this year. A bunch of us need to set up."

Heads around the class nod.

Sawyer crosses to my side of the room, and when he looks up at me it's the closest I've been to him in days.

"Do you know how much a class costs at this institution?"

"A lot."

"But you don't know how much. Because your parents pay for it."

I ignore his digging. "Some people would say the most important lessons are learned outside the classroom."

"You're going to learn more from hanging banners than in my class?"

There's a dangerous edge to his voice. But it's been a rough week, and I'm tired of being the one to act like an adult in the face of people who won't.

I shrug, glancing at the clock. "Maybe."

"Then don't let me keep you." Sawyer crosses

to the door and holds it wide.

The room has gone silent. All eyes are on me.

I grab my bag and head for the door.

"My office. After class," he mutters as I brush past him.

My bare thigh bounces on the bench outside Sawyer's office. He's keeping me waiting on purpose.

If this is some kind of lesson, it's not going to work.

I've been there ten minutes when my stomach growls.

I pull out the apple I packed, and am about to bite into it when he saunters down the hall.

"How nice of you to show up," I comment.

"Had something to do." He unlocks the door and I follow him in.

He rounds the desk and sets his books on the top before lifting that scorching gaze up my body —slow—finally settling on my face.

"Why do you want to go to this dance?"

Every inch of him is tight, and the softness in his voice sets me back. "You called me in here to ask that?"

"If I'm considering letting you out early for

the event, I'd like to understand what I'm letting you out early for."

"I'm on the dance committee. We handled everything from logistics to ticket sales to decorations. Plus Fall Ball is a charity event, so there's a silent auction and sponsorships. It's our job to make sure it looks perfect."

I turn the apple in my hand, admiring its gleaming, red, unbroken surface.

"Perfect is overrated." His mouth twitches, but I shake my head. There's no way he'd understand this.

"Shitty-looking auction tables don't get good bids. Besides, I've had my dress for ages."

I cross to the bookshelves, running a finger over the spines.

"I understand there's been some fallout from the video taken at the club, despite its removal from R.U. DOWN," he says. "I trust that's what this"—I glance over and he nods to my outfit—"is about."

I shrug. He's trying to get under my skin and I'm not in the mood for it. "Just felt like a change."

None of the books I lent Lancaster appear to be here, so I take a step toward the next shelf. It also brings me closer to Sawyer.

"You were going to end up in a wrestling match with Attwood."

"And?"

"And he'd enjoy it too damn much." Sawyer leans an elbow on the back of his chair. "If you want to dress like that, don't do it for them. Do it for you."

I turn to face him, the bookshelves forgotten. "Tell me you didn't call me in here for some weak PSA."

I lift the apple to my lips, my teeth breaking its skin. Sweetness flows into my mouth, and I watch him watch me as I reach up to wipe away a spot of juice from the corner of my mouth. "Are we done here?"

Sawyer's gaze heats.

There are rules for my relationships with everyone in my life: my parents, Adam. With my professor, those rules have been broken, leaving tantalizing emptiness in their place.

I'm halfway out of the room before he calls, "We're not done. Shut the door."

His voice has dropped an octave in an instant. Whatever thoughts he was thinking have turned undeniably darker.

I grip the apple harder. I should walk away, but I want his attention. I crave it.

The door clicks closed, and my heart starts to race as I turn back to him.

"We are not equal," he murmurs, rounding the desk. Every muscle is taut. "You are not my colleague. Not my girlfriend. You are in my class."

"Is that why you haven't shaved in two days? You're too busy preparing scintillating lectures on mechanical components? Which, by the way, are identical to Lancaster's. You might want to put in more effort given all the money our parents are paying for your class."

His gaze narrows. "Stop."

I lick my lips, glancing back at the door. "Make me."

Since I met him, I'm less compliant than I was, less inclined to follow whatever rules the world set for me.

With him, I can feel the thrill of saying what I want, and being a brat without repercussions.

Except the look in his eye says there are about to be repercussions.

"I have a lesson for you. Learn it, and you can take Friday's quiz early and skip class."

I raise a brow. "Can't wait."

Whatever test he wants to give me, I can handle it. I'm up to date on the readings. Each graph on my most recent lab report has been triple checked. I could probably pass the midterm even though we haven't finished all of the material yet, and—

"Elbows on the desk."

My heart stops.

He gestures to the surface as if he's offering me a cup of coffee and not a place to lie down in front of his hungry eyes.

Asking him to repeat it isn't an option. It's clear from his expression that what I heard is exactly what he intended to say. When he reaches for the cuffs on his shirt to roll up one sleeve and then the other, my pulse stutters back to life.

I could walk out of this room without a backward glance. No one but us would know if I deleted Sawyer Redmond from my phone and never spoke to him again except when I'm surrounded by a classroom of engineering students.

But I don't want to give in. And if I leave, I won't find out where this leads.

He holds out a hand for the apple. With a moment's hesitation, I relinquish it.

Shifting my weight forward, I place my arms on the smooth wood desk.

He steps behind me, close enough I get a hit of his addictive scent.

His hand brushes the back of my bare thigh. I have a sudden urge to press back against him. But the second I move, he steadies me with a hand on my hip.

His touch travels up my skin, teasing, assessing.

My body throbs. I want to squeeze my legs together because this ache is getting intolerable fast.

"Wider." He kicks the inside of my ankle, and I step further apart without thinking. Sawyer's dress shoes appear on the carpet between my feet.

I want him to touch me like he did last week. I need the adrenaline, the feeling like I can do anything and be anything.

"You liked telling that kid he can't get you off," he says.

"Standing up for myself isn't a crime. If that's what this is about—"

"In my class, I make the rules. Now lift your skirt or I'll do it for you."

I nearly die. The idea of what he might do after makes my hands fist on the desk.

But we're in his office. There's no way he'll take this further. He might be reckless, but he's not insane.

"Then do it," I dare him.

All of a sudden, cool air hits my thighs. The fabric of my skirt tickles my strip of bare waist as I stretch over the desk.

I'm standing in the middle of his office, exposed to his gaze.

"You walked away from me the other day," he growls. "I need to know whether it was because you don't want this, or because you don't want to want it."

I don't know what "this" means, but I want it more than anything I've experienced in my twenty years.

I swallow, a vein pounding painfully in my forehead. "It doesn't matter what I want. We can't."

"On the contrary. What you want is the only thing that matters."

The laughter of students on the path outside the engineering building drifts through the crack in the window.

They might as well be miles away.

When he grabs the side of my panties and drags them down... they're forgotten altogether.

He squeezes my ass with a rough hand, and it feels so good. My eyes shut and when I arch back into his touch, he doesn't try to stop me.

The low sound from behind me could be a groan.

"Every word you said was true," he murmurs. "He can't get you off. Neither can that ex of yours. Because neither of them sees who you really are."

Sawyer brushes a finger right next to my center. Pleasure shoots through me, leaving my knees trembling.

Yes. More.

But as soon as he's there, he's gone.

"Lift your feet."

I do, each in turn and only half aware of what's happening.

The next second, the hem of my skirt tickles my thighs again as Sawyer flips it back down.

"Good. You can leave."

Confusion has my brain glitching. I flex my sweaty palms on the desk before shoving off it to face him.

"You're joking." I'm pissed off from the confrontation with Remi, turned on from arguing with him, and he expects me to walk out the door like this? "It's windy. And I have two more classes today."

Sawyer balls up the fabric of my panties and tucks it in the breast pocket of his jacket. "You should've thought of that sooner."

I tug down my skirt, trying to cover more of

myself and failing. "You want everyone on campus to see me."

"I want you to take ownership of your actions." His dark eyes flash. "When you danced on stage at Velvet, you acted like a woman who owned her choices. Then you retreated back into your shell. You're better than that."

Sawyer reaches past me for the door, opening it with a soft click.

"Here." He sets the apple back in my palm, bite marks facing up. "You look famished."

11

OLIVIA

"*D*ammit. Can I use the straightener?" Jules calls from the bathroom.

"Second drawer," Kat shouts back as I zip up her red cocktail dress. "I thought you were wearing your hair up?"

"That was the plan. It's rebelling."

Kat lunges across the room for her Solo cup and we head out to the living room.

"AGHHH!!" Jules stands in barefoot in a simple green sheath, wild-eyed. Her hair is half pinned on her head, chunks sticking out in every direction.

My dance recital experience kicks in faster than you can say "bobby pins."

"Hey. We can get through this." I squeeze in to the bathroom behind her, the taffeta layers of my black floor-length gown crunching as I slide through the door. "You want it up?"

"Yeah." Jules huffs out a breath. "But it was supposed to look more like this." She makes wave-like motions at the front of her head, and a smooth stroke across the back.

"Then that's what we'll do."

Kat sticks her head in the door, reaching for her perfume bottle on the counter. "You didn't want to go with her tonight?"

Jules wrinkles her nose. "No. I need to keep you guys out of trouble."

I feel for my roommate. She's had an on-again, off-again thing with a girl since freshman year. I want to shake the other girl and tell her to get her shit together, because Jules is smart and kind and anyone would be lucky to have her.

Half an hour later, we're ready.

My phone buzzes on the counter.

Emma: Send me pictures from Fall Ball!

I text her back a selfie of the three of us posing in our dresses.

Emma: UGH! I'm jealous.

Emma: We were supposed to go to Josie's

parents' place in Tuscany for her birthday this weekend but Mom made up some lame excuse and won't let me.

Weird. Mom loves for Emma to socialize with Josie, whose family has more vineyards than children.

Unless Dad's company's problems are bigger than he let on, and he didn't want to spring for part of a charter flight and a birthday present to match.

I shove the family drama from my mind. Tonight I want enjoy the result of our hard work.

Fall Ball is on campus at the University Center, so we decide to walk.

If there was any question whether tonight was special, it's obvious the moment you catch sight of the building.

Strings of fairy lights gild the trees, whose leaves have turned burnt oranges and yellows in the fall.

Inside, there are more fairy lights, plus gold balloons and decorations from tiers of pumpkins painted white, black, and gold.

Hundreds of students already line the room, and music drifts from the band in one corner.

My heart lifts. It's really beautiful.

Adam and some other guys ambush us when we arrive.

My ex greets me with a purple orchid corsage. "For you."

"Cheesy," Kat informs him.

He smoothly flips her off.

"Adam, I'm not here with you," I say.

"But I saw this and it made me think of you. It's like the one I got you for prom, remember? If you won't wear it, then a perfectly good flower died for nothing." He slips it on my wrist.

Whatever. It's a flower, not an engagement ring.

The band chafes and I adjust it. A pin scratches my skin, a bead of blood appearing moments later. I press my hand to the tiny wound.

When I look up, my gaze locks on a man on the other side of the crowd.

Sawyer Redmond is gorgeous in a dark suit cut to fit his sharp shoulders and lean hips. His hair loose around his face, he's ruthless, and almost painfully beautiful.

Did he come to see me?

The thought is strangely romantic, until I see a stunning woman in a fitted silver cocktail dress cross to him and whisper in his ear.

I duck through the crowd, heading for the

bar. I grab a gold napkin off a stack of them and press it to my wrist.

"Using your fake ID again, I see," a familiar voice comments from behind me.

"Is this the realtor again?" I can't resist asking as Sawyer orders a water. "The only bedroom she's interested in selling is hers. To you."

He gets his water and turns back to the crowd of dancers. We're standing a respectable distance apart, not looking at each other, but neither of us moves.

"Faculty don't usually bring dates," I inform him.

"She invited herself. And I'm new."

"Meaning you don't know how things are done."

"Meaning I don't give a shit how things are done."

His flash of teeth makes my heart skip.

I'm thrown back to lying across his desk, him flipping up my skirt and palming my ass and dragging down my underwear.

My gaze flicks to his jacket pocket as if I expect to see the fabric peeking out.

Before I can answer, a guy from the organizing committee wearing a suit and a panicked expression flags me down.

"Olivia! There's an emergency in the dining area."

I head that way without hesitating.

The normal seating has been removed for tonight's event, replaced by long tables filled with every kind of treat imaginable.

At the center is a three-tiered chocolate fountain. Dark rivers spill over the concentric circles, but there's steam coming up from the middle and there are chunks in the glossy candy.

"It's overheating," I mutter to no one.

"The bigger problem is who put it next to the ice sculpture?"

I spin to see Sawyer behind me, surveying the scene in amusement.

I bite my cheek to keep from laughing. "Hey. We had some very dedicated volunteers who spent all day setting up."

I duck under the tablecloth to unplug the fountain.

Sawyer's there with an extended hand when I rise.

"Thanks," I murmur.

"You and your friends spent all day working on this. Why?"

"We spent all day and half of this week and planning for the past six months," I correct. "We met after Fall Ball in our first year. Adam and I were arguing about something. I needed air and went outside. I ducked behind the tree out front and tripped over Jules, who was sitting on the ground. She'd brought a date, this girl she hit it off with in orientation week, but it turned out she was just using Jules for attention." *She still does*, I don't say. "Then Kat showed up in a ballgown with a flask, and the rest is history."

"You were in the same program."

"No."

"Same dorm?"

I shake my head. "We were just random atoms colliding. And we never separated."

His eyes soften. "Have you always taken care of everyone?"

His description makes my brows lift. "If you can do something to make another person's life a tiny bit better, wouldn't you?"

He cocks his head, looking around. "When I was an undergrad, this was smaller. Less of a spectacle."

"I'm surprised you came. You don't seem like the school spirit type."

"I wasn't. But all the girls came. And even if dating wasn't my thing, I always liked sex."

His wolfish smile could melt panties for miles. But more than that, I'm having fun with him. We're talking like two normal people. No agenda except enjoying each other's presence.

"And that was how you dealt with pressure. Sex." My attention shifts to a platter of strawberries on the table so I don't lose myself in his eyes. "What do you need a pressure release from now?"

"A new project with a former rival. We're going into business together next year."

I grab a strawberry and freeze with it halfway to my lips. "The same thing you were doing with your old company?"

He shoots me a look, as if he's not going to answer, but relents. "We were immensely successful, and on the way to bigger things still. One tracking mod I built from the ground up secured eight figures in government funding, and private companies were banging down the door to buy from us after we commercialized it."

Damn. Guys my age beat their chest for scoring a decent internship, but my professor has made huge achievements as a student and in industry. It's admirable, and sexy.

I pop the berry into my mouth, thinking as I chew and swallow. "And that's what did it for you? The money?"

"The money didn't suck, but no, that didn't 'do it for me.'" His mouth twitches. "We worked on applications from space exploration to medical devices. Landing a rover on a lake on Mars or performing surgery on premature babies. It will all be infinitely attainable with the right combination of human ingenuity and problem solving."

He's beautiful and utterly confident, but more than that, his determination is addictive.

"So if it works, what then? I mean…" I go on at his incredulous look, "We can conquer the moon, but what happens to what we leave behind? We conquer something, we stop looking after it."

"Like what?"

It takes no time to come up with an example. "The fish in Lancaster's tank. Their habitats are being eroded."

"And you care because…"

"I know what it's like to be what's left behind." I play with the flower on my wrist, its natural beauty at odds with the modern building. "Engineers are smart. But they spend more time asking 'how' than 'why.' Maybe they should ask why more often."

"Perhaps they should." His gaze lingers on me, intensifying as I grab another berry and bite into it.

"It's Regal Plum."

"Excuse me?"

"My lipstick," I murmur, emboldened by the fact that we're in public, on as close to neutral ground as possible. "You're staring at my mouth, so I figured you wanted to know what color my lipstick was."

"Could be. Or, it could be I'm remembering you lying across my desk, your panties in my pocket and your mouth sticky from that apple."

In an instant, I'm flushed everywhere.

"But you're probably right. I'm sure it was the lipstick thing." He smirks.

Two students wheel a table of crowns and sashes toward the stage.

"Fall Ball court," I manage, recovering.

"That's what the voting was on the way in."

I nod. "There's a short list every year based on service and popularity. We should probably go that way."

We're nearly back to the other room when the speakers crackle to life.

The university administrator on stage begins to announce the court. We watch as the first two students go up and accept their recognition.

"So pretty do-gooders parading around for attention." He snorts. "Hard pass."

"For contributions to the Fall Ball organizing committee...Olivia Barclay."

Sawyer laughs silently beside me. "They must've voted before the chocolate fountain started smoking."

I flip him off, which only elicits a bigger grin.

"Get your do-gooding ass up there."

I make my way up to the stage, spotting Kat with a group of classmates on the way. She winks gleefully. Probably stuffed the ballot box.

The woman handing out awards sets the crown on my head, but as I smile at the crowd of students, it feels empty.

After, there's a dance for all members of the court.

Someone taps my shoulder, and I turn to find Adam. "Come on. You're not gonna dance alone, are you?"

I lift my hand to his and place the other around his neck. We move around the dance floor to the music, the corsage itching my wrist as we move.

After a few turns around the floor, Adam pulls me closer.

"You look incredible," he murmurs, an appreciative expression on his face. "I miss seeing your face."

"You see me in class, and for the design project."

"But it's not the same."

I let myself get caught up in his deep blue eyes. He's always been handsome and charming. Since high school, half the female class and some of the guys wanted him. Back then, I was honored he took an interest in me.

"I wish I could see you more." He pauses. "I told Coach I can't be pulling extra practices around the clock. I want to take you out."

"That's sweet, Adam, but—"

"You don't have time now," he finishes. "I respect what you're doing with the team. But I told you, I can get you a spot at our company. Let Royce be the smart one and Madison be the driven one." I stiffen and he plows on. "Or, if you don't want to do engineering, you can do whatever you want."

"So we get a tux and a white dress and book a five-star hotel for hundreds of our closest friends? Toast to a future like our parents' past? Because you know that's what my mom wants."

"Come on. You've never pictured it? You'd look gorgeous. You *are* gorgeous."

"But what happens after the wedding day?"

"We go on like we have been." He frowns. "It's a good life, Liv. Whoever or whatever's got you thinking it isn't is dead wrong."

Could I do what my mom wanted? Put myself

on the line to give security to not only myself but our family?

I always enjoyed the way Adam held me—steady, easy. As if the room revolved around me, if not his world. But now, I'm searching the crowd over his shoulder.

After the dance, I'm on my way back from the bathroom when someone grabs me and drags me past a row of coats into a semi-dark service hallway.

"Why do you let him look at you like that?"

The light overhead flickers. My pulse accelerates as I stare up into my professor's reckless face. "I can't control how people look at me."

"You spend enough time trying. You're locked into a dance, and not the one happening on the floor." He brushes a thumb over my lower lip. "I bet you suck him off with that perfect mouth, and thank him after for the privilege."

I slap his hand away. "And you wish it was you."

He's vibrating with intensity, and when I look down, his pants are tented.

It's true.

He might hate my dress and my hair and the fact that I try to follow the rules, but he wants me.

I'm not a toy to be forgotten and discarded

like with Adam, or a chess piece to be used like with my family.

"Tell me you've thought about it," I whisper.

On the other side of coatcheck, the sounds of The Weeknd stream through the speakers as the party rages on.

My professor's hand trails down my neck. His touch skims over the cleavage exposed by my dress, dipping between my breasts to yank me closer.

"I met a woman at a club. She was brave and sexy, and yeah, I thought about how much fun we could have. But you? You're a scared girl and you proved it again tonight. So dance all you want with that 'gentleman' of yours. I don't want anything from you."

Sawyer and I can't be together.

He knows how futile this is, and yet, he's here with me.

I fuck him up every bit as much as he does me, and right now, I need that twisted reciprocity.

But if I do this, everything changes.

School is about trying new things and finding out who I am. I don't want to leave as the same girl who arrived.

The floor is dusty. I adjust my skirt before sinking to my knees.

"What are you doing?" Sawyer's voice is raw.

The coarse fabric of my dress rubs my bare legs as I reach under his jacket. My fingers shake as I flick the button on his pants open and work the zipper down over his thick, rigid cock encased in black boxer briefs.

I tug the waistband down enough to wrap my hand around him, his shaft like steel and satin, and his jaw clenches.

"Cherry..."

He's going to tell me to stop. But when issues a raw command, it's not the one I expect.

"Open your mouth."

It's on.

Every second with this man is a challenge, a thrill, but instead of running away I want to squeeze my eyes shut and hold on tight.

He rubs his cock over my lips, the slick precum sticking to my skin. It's beyond sexy, knowing he's so turned on. That I'm the cause of it.

I shift forward, eager to wrap my lips around him, stretching to fit him in. The instant I succeed, he groans his approval.

He's huge and silky on my tongue. My thighs squeeze at the thought of what I'm doing, what we're doing.

"Relax." He brushes my jaw, and I try. The

moment my mouth opens wider, he slides deeper on a shaky inhale. "*Fuck*, yes. Now suck me."

I suck until my cheeks hollow.

His shallow breathing is the best reward. His fingers twist in my hair, yanking hard enough my scalp hurts. "You're so fucking sweet. I need more. Tell me I can have your mouth."

I'm not sure what he means but he's so reverent, I try to nod.

Sawyer takes the crown off my head and slips the edge under the top of my dress, rubbing the plastic across my swollen nipple. The lazy way he does it to get a response makes me shudder.

"He's going to walk you to your door tonight. Try to kiss you, because he wants to win you back, but knows you're not going to let him fuck you."

I shift on my knees, trying to pull away but he fists his hand in my hair.

He pulls the crown out of my dress, tosses it down the hall.

"You're going to feel me when he does."

He drags my head back, slides further down my throat. My gag reflex kicks in and his eyes darken.

He won't hurt me. I trust him.

When he starts to thrust, his grip is relentless, holding my neck and head while he fucks me. I try to relax my jaw, let him slide down my tongue.

If I wind up with strep throat, I'm demanding an extension on my class deadlines, Professor Redmond.

The thought makes me giggle. Which, in our current position, makes me choke.

He pulls out immediately. "What the...Are you laughing?"

I try to hide my grin. "No."

Sawyer curses. "What am I going to do with you, Cherry?"

He sounds genuinely bewildered as he leans back against the wall, shoving a hand through his sweat-damp hair.

My gaze drops to the steel rod between us.

"Oh, don't worry. We're definitely doing that," he promises. His husky voice is tinged with humor but the words are a warning.

I open my mouth obediently, and he slides back in. This time his fingers sift through my hair. He's caressing me, not gripping me.

His strokes grow faster, shallower, and when I feel him tighten, I barely have time to inhale once before he's coming down my throat.

I swallow the endless stream of him, transfixed by the way his head is thrown back, jaw clenched and eyes dark slits of awe and approval.

I'm on my knees, yet it's the biggest high I've ever felt.

Before I can recover, voices sound down the hall.

I shove off my knees and he helps me scramble to standing, moments before a group of drunk students stumbles around the rack of coats toward us. I turn my back toward them and hold my breath until they're past.

I want so much more, but we can't. It's lucky we weren't caught.

My stomach rumbles, catching us both by surprise.

"Did you eat dinner? Other than strawberries," Sawyer demands, and I shake my head.

"We were too busy getting ready. Maybe I'll grab a shrimp cocktail."

He frowns. "Eat something. But not the shrimp. Daniel got food poisoning from them one year."

I roll my eyes. "I don't know where your Fall Ball committee got their seafood back in the day, but I assure you our suppliers are excellent."

Sawyer adjusts his pants, tucking his shirt back in with a mocking expression. "Back in the day? It was ten years ago, not a generation."

His exasperation makes me grin. "Any good memories of Fall Ball?"

"I stole a bunch of cutlery and superglued it to Lancaster's fence."

I laugh as I straighten his suit. His grin fades but his eyes stay warm.

"Ready to go back out there?"

"Mm-hmm. If Adam kisses me, I'll tell him I have strep throat."

Sawyer snorts. "Text me when you get home tonight."

"It's the weekend. You're off duty, Professor."

He catches me by my wrist, pressing the wound that's stopped bleeding. "I mean it. Let me know you got home safe."

OLIVIA

Liv: I'm home.

Unknown: Send me a photo.

I finish brushing my teeth, then open my mouth and take a picture of the inside and hit send.

Unknown: What the fuck is that?

Liv: I thought you meant to check that my throat wasn't irreparably damaged.

Unknown: For that, you'll text me every night this week.

I grin.

Madison, Royce, and I meet up in the design lab on Monday. Adam bailed citing basketball practice, but I'm relieved after Fall Ball.

"Have you seen the other projects that won in past years?" I hold out my phone. "They're really advanced."

"Right now ours is no better than an arm moving up and down," Madison gripes from her spot on one of the stools.

"At least it's not shattering chips anymore," Royce points out from across the lab bench.

"We have less than a month to get this working to qualify our prototype. An arm is fine," I continue, "but there are lots of double- or triple-jointed robots out there already." After getting through Sawyer's pile of research papers and our conversation the other night, I started reading more broadly. "What if we built something with better articulation? Something inspired by nature?"

Madison sits silent, her gaze fixed on the lab counter.

Royce leans over and snaps his fingers in front of her. "Hey. You there?"

She shifts back on her stool. "What're you thinking...a tail?"

I lean in. "With more joints and more range of motion, it could perform more complex tasks."

I'm getting swept up in the possibilities. I get what Sawyer was talking about at Fall Ball: the high that comes from creating a masterpiece that moves and responds and solves problems of its own.

"We'd need more budget for materials, and extra lab time but I can text—I mean email— Professor Redmond."

Madison groans loudly and Royce looks between us.

"I'm gonna give you five." He grabs his phone and heads for the door.

"Royce!" Madison shouts. "What the hell?"

He flashes a peace sign over his shoulder, then disappears.

Madison and I are alone.

"When the video from Velvet was posted, I thought you were in the right place at the right time to see it," I say at last. "But I'm not sure that's true." Her reaction wasn't so much surprised delight, but satisfaction. "You're the one who posted it."

She slaps her notebook loudly on the table-top. "I'm not admitting to anything."

She did it. I know she did.

I pace the room before turning back. "Why do you hate me?"

Madison flips both palms in the air. "I don't hate you!" I wait her out. "You don't even want to be here. For the first two years, you were like an extension of your boyfriend. Yet professors *always* notice you. Last year with Lancaster, I asked to be his research assistant. He said he wasn't taking anyone on, but you were around him all the time. And it's even worse with Redmond."

Guilt edges into my righteousness. But there's no reason for it to—it's not like Sawyer gives me special treatment. Does he?

"Do you know how many women are in our year of engineering?" I ask.

"Twelve."

"Out of sixty students," I confirm. "You posting that video for everyone? It was deliberate and it hurt me." Her gaze drops to the floor. "I don't want to fight with you. But you're making it damned hard not to."

Liv: I need something, and you're the only one who can give it to me.

Unknown: If you beg, I'll think about it. Tell me what you want, Cherry.

Liv: Five more hours a week of DL for the next month.

Unknown: You want me to get you lab time?!?

Liv: Pretty please? I want it, Professor.

Liv: I need it so badly.

Liv: Only you can give it to me.

Unknown: You're being ridiculous.

Liv: Is it working? ;)

Unknown: I checked the schedule and moved a few things around. I can get you three extra hours a week. But you better still be sleeping and eating.

"Bullseye," Jules croons as the dart lands in the center of the board.

She high-fives Kat before dropping onto the

stool across the table at our bar. "Bet you can't match that."

"I'll take that bet," I decide, grabbing the darts and setting up. "If I win, I get the rest of your six-pack of yogurt in the fridge."

"Weird," Kat comments.

"I haven't had time to go grocery shopping this week."

"Which is why we're here," Jules points out.

The week has flown by thanks to assignments, labs, and tying up loose ends from Fall Ball.

I've seen Sawyer in lectures, and once in his office with a string of students behind me in the open doorway waiting their turn.

After what went down between us, not being alone with him is brutal. Texting him every night reminds me he's close, but he feels so far away.

Now that it's Friday, my roommates dragged me out for dinner and drinks.

"Homecoming's next weekend," Jules reminds us and I groan.

"My parents are coming. We need to do the whole song and dance."

"But Emma will be here, right?"

"Yeah, at least there's that."

We head home from the bar arm in arm.

When I trip in the door, tugging off my boots, my phone rings.

"Ignore it. We need to watch a movie," Kat demands.

When I finish fighting with my boot and take in the number on the screen, I shiver with anticipation. "In a bit. Start without me."

I'm breathless when I make it into my room.

"Hi, you," I answer.

"Are you drunk?" Sawyer's voice is surprised.

"A little. Just went out with my roommates."

At the sound of the TV and my roommates laughing, I shut the door quietly behind me.

"And forgot to text me."

"I didn't forget." The buzz from the alcohol is still going strong in my veins. "I wanted to put it off. I hate saying good night to you."

"Tough. You earned it."

"No, I mean...I like talking to you. But I want to talk to you all night."

He's quiet, and I wonder if I was too candid. "All right, let's talk."

I grab my earbud headphones off my night-stand, sticking them in. "Why did you leave New York this summer?"

"Do you always ask difficult questions when you're inebriated?"

"It's a normal question. Sue me for being

curious about the guy I text every night." I smile as I pad back toward the door, the carpet tickling my bare feet.

Even his sigh is delicious. "A disagreement with my co-founder. He went to great lengths to excise me from my own company."

"How is that possible? Your name must have been on everything."

"I gave it up."

"But I thought you loved your work."

"The work, yes. The people were disloyal and self-interested. Now, I hope this isn't what you wanted to talk about, because we're done this line of conversation."

I want to press, but I sense he'll shut down if I do. And more than anything, I want to keep talking to him.

"I'm glad you came to Russell to cover your dad's classes." I peer at the trees outside my window. "You told me that night outside your car that you didn't regret meeting me. I don't regret meeting you, either."

The next sigh is even better. "I wish we'd met under different circumstances. You are the last person I should be spending time with."

"Because you're my professor."

Sawyer doesn't answer, and for a moment I wonder if there's more to it than that.

Which is nuts, because that's more than enough of a problem already.

"Come on," I tease, "messy hall blowjobs at university-sanctioned events aren't your thing?"

His soft chuckle is my reward. "They are utterly my thing."

"Knew it." My smile fades. "But if we were caught, you could lose your teaching job." I think of the money he's vowed to commit to foster kids.

"It's bigger than that, Olivia."

I straighten. "Bigger how?"

His soft curse sounds louder in the earbud headphones. "Forget it. I'm tired."

I slip out of my room, going to the kitchen for a glass of water. Kat and Jules gesture from the living room and I hold up a finger.

"You're working too much," I say, as quiet as I can to keep from being overheard. "Going through your dad's things, plus lecturing, plus working on whatever projects you're planning—"

"What I need is for a certain girl to take better care of herself, and text me earlier in the evening so I'm not up worrying about her ass."

His tone changes, but I'm wound so tight and he's unquestionably the reason for it. I want to know him, but I also just *want* him, and it's impossible to disentangle the two.

"Because after you text me, you go right to sleep," I taunt.

I return to my room with the glass of water, chugging half of it on the way. Then kick the door shut with my foot.

"Did you take my underwear to punish me? Or so you could rub yourself and think of me? Because if it's the second, you should've given me a heads-up. I would've worn something softer. Lace, maybe."

"You're not as innocent as you pretend to be, Cherry. You look like a flower, but you go off like a bomb."

I laugh under my breath, but the idea of Sawyer using my panties to jerk off is obscenely sexy.

"Are you lying down?" he asks.

"No. I'm leaning against my door, ready to spring into action."

"What kind of action? It's late and you're drunk."

"All kinds of action. You underestimate me."

"I'm the only person who doesn't." The words send a ripple of pleasure through me.

I shift back, my heart thudding as I stare up at the ceiling. My skin tingles, and my fingers drift across my stomach under my T-shirt, up across my breasts. "I wish you were here."

"Fuck, so do I. Only then, you'd get no sleep at all."

"I probably won't sleep tonight anyway," I murmur. "Thinking about you, talking to you... it does something to me."

"Cherry." His voice is heavy and full.

"Yeah."

"Pull down your panties. Tell me once you've done it."

It's as if he said the words against my throat, low enough I could feel them in my breasts, my fingertips. Anticipation shimmers across my skin, dances in the air.

"Okay," I whisper, working the fabric down over my hips.

"Good. Now spread your thighs."

I push my thong the rest of the way down, kicking it off my ankle so I can widen my knees. Cool air tickles my skin and my heart races.

"Lick your finger, then rub yourself bare."

I swallow hard. Sawyer's in my ears, in my head, telling me to touch myself.

This can't be real.

But until some alarm blares to jerk me out of my fantasy-driven dream, I'm going along with it.

I slide my hand down my stomach, my thighs already trembling before my fingers find my slick skin.

"Ohh." The world goes dark as my eyelids shut. "That feels good."

His laugh is wicked. "I bet you're slick."

"Don't think it has anything to do with you," I say, breathless. "I watched some very titillating *Jeopardy* earlier."

"Intellectual older men are your type?"

"I don't believe in types. Do you? It means you don't see a person for who they are."

"Keep going, Cherry Bomb."

I bite my cheek against the moan as the contact sends pleasure radiating through me. My knees shake. "I need to lie down."

"No. You need to come."

I swallow. It's hot, what he's suggesting, but... "I don't think I can."

"I felt you come on my fingers in the middle of the street against my car," he reminds me, his voice warming. "If you need an audience—"

"That's not it."

"Do you have a vibrator?"

My heart skips, a flush crawling up my cheeks. "Yes."

"Get it."

I reach for my nightstand and pull out a slim vibe that's my go-to, then return to the door, my reflection in the mirror barely registering.

An eager woman wearing a tank top and nothing else.

"Now slip it inside."

Under his command, I do just that.

I feel my body make room for the toy. My breath trembles out as I clench around it.

"Now turn it on," he says.

"My roommates are outside."

"Do it, Olivia."

My fingers turn the dial on the end, and the low vibration sends me to another level.

A wave of heat rolls through me and I arch my back, my shoulders digging into the wood.

It's Sawyer inside me, making me feel this way. Hungry, desperate, aching, wanting...

"Tell me how good it is."

My free hand skims up my body, rubbing my breast. "So good."

I'm getting close.

"I need you to remember something," he murmurs.

"What's that?"

"This is nothing like how it'll be when I fuck you."

Every part of me goes tight—my stomach, my thighs, my chest, my toes.

"*OhmyGod.*" Pleasure radiates from my core, a violent wave that grips me. I squeeze hard around the toy, twisting and writhing as my release tears through me, wave after wave.

I take out the toy and slide down the door, boneless, until my ass hits the carpet.

My head drops back against the wood panel. My heart hammers in my ears, gradually slowing along with the sounds of his breathing.

"Olivia. Think you can sleep now?"

I blow the hair out of my face. "I don't know if I'll ever be able to sleep again."

His tight chuckle makes me smile as I hold up the sex toy and remember taking him in my mouth at Fall Ball.

He's definitely bigger than this.

Like, a lot.

"You really want to fuck me?" I blurt.

"More than anything."

I've never had someone want me with that kind of intensity. With Adam or other guys in school, I've always felt interchangeable. With Sawyer, it's as if he sees straight to the heart of me. Like any other girl would be insufficient.

"But," he goes on, "I need you ready first."

What does that mean?

He speaks before I can ask.

"We're doing my father's service on Saturday."

I scramble up to sitting. "Homecoming weekend."

"That's when his colleagues could fly in."

My parents will be here, too, for the pep rally and the game the next day. It's the worst possible time, but I'm not letting Lancaster or Sawyer down.

"I'll be there."

13

SAWYER

"Thanks for the help," I say as Daniel arrives with a truck full of two-by-fours. The realtor suggested shoring up the flower beds in the front, and when my friend saw me outside measuring, he insisted on being part of it.

"No problem. Though given how you fell through the porch, I'm pretty sure this place has bigger issues than the landscaping before you sell it. You get in touch with any of the contractors I sent you?"

"Yeah, but I think I'm going to do the outside myself."

He shrugs. "Your call."

As Daniel and I set to work digging a trench

around the flower bed, it's hard to explain why I don't want to contract all the work out.

Maybe because this place is my problem and I'm going to deal with it.

"You all set for the service?" he asks after we've edged the border and cut wood to fit.

"I pulled out some of his old pictures." Trying to find stuff for the funeral made me appreciate how much shit he had. Books, papers, mechanical components, and computer chips.

His lawyer contacted me about the will, saying the majority of his assets were left to me but a few things weren't.

I didn't ask the details, because I didn't want to know.

I nod to the fence, and one spot that still has the outline of a fork in the paint. "You remember when we did that?"

"Fuck yeah. Hope Fall Ball's got new cutlery."

"They seem to. I went last week."

Daniel wipes the sweat from his forehead with the back of his arm. "Sounds like a terrible way to spend a Friday evening."

"My realtor wanted to meet up over dinner to talk. I told her I had another commitment. She invited herself along."

I start toward the pile of cut wood.

"So the thing with Olivia," Daniel calls. "That's over?"

A strangled sound, half laugh and half groan, rips from my throat. "It's not over."

Ever since Olivia Barclay sucked me off in the hallway on her knees, I haven't been able to think of anything else.

It was unexpected. I was pissed at her, at that kid Adam who goes through life like he deserves everything.

I shouldn't have told her to text me every night, but I wanted to hear her voice. Or at least her words.

When she called me last night, the temptation was too much to resist.

I didn't tell her I was stroking myself too, that her sounds as she came gave me enough material to fuck my hand to for days. Weeks.

She's innocent and seductive at the same time. I want to bury myself inside her, to watch every thought of perfection drift away when she realizes...

Messy is better than perfect.

Feeling is better than numbness.

The line between control and anarchy isn't just blurry...straddling it is the only way to live.

I told myself I wanted to break her down, but I also want to build her up. I want to watch her succeed, want her to see she's stronger than she knows.

"She's a bad idea," Daniel says as I return, laying two pieces of wood at a ninety degree angle in the trench we built.

"No one's going to get hurt." I hold out a hand for the hammer, and he passes it to me.

"Like no one got hurt in New York?"

The first swing, I hit my thumb as well as the nail and suck in a breath. "That was different."

"If you say so." Something light hits me in the back of the head, and I whip around to see Daniel holding a handful of soil and wearing a grin. I shake my head, but it's impossible to stay mad.

"Save some for the garden, yeah?"

We return to work, securing the frame in place. After years in New York, it feels good to work with my hands instead of only my head.

"It must be a weight off your mind to have this done on the weekend," he says when we're ready to add topsoil.

"Was it after your wife's funeral?"

"Yes and no. Andy's grandparents made things even more difficult. We got through it but I'm not sure we would have without you." Daniel rips open a bag and dumps it into the bed. "The way you intervened? It could have gone a lot worse. They wanted to take my kid from me, Sawyer."

It's impossible to hide the anguish in his voice.

I rock back on my heels. "I wasn't gonna watch that happen. There's no better dad in the world for Andy than you."

Daniel's face relaxes into a smile. "I hope you find someone you love like I loved her."

I shake my head. "Don't take this the wrong way, but no thanks. I watched what you went through. I don't need that."

"How old were you when your mom died? Seven?"

"Six." The tightening in my chest catches me by surprise.

His eyes search mine, unreadable for once. "It's okay to be sick of losing people, Sawyer. Doesn't make you weak. Makes you human."

14

OLIVIA

"**W**here are you going dressed like that?" Kat asks from the kitchen.

"Lancaster's funeral." I check my makeup in the mirror by the front door and smooth a hand over my sleek, low ponytail.

"Shit, I forgot. So you're going to go to that instead of the basketball game?"

"I'll go to both."

My mom called to say they'd be here mid-afternoon ahead of the exhibition game.

I settled on the black short-sleeved dress with a high collar since I won't have time to change between the service and meeting my parents for dinner before the game.

Kat appears behind me in the mirror, wrapping her arms around my shoulders.

"Ahhh!" I screech. "Don't touch me with those."

She holds her hands—still wet with bits of clay from her latest project—away from my body. "I'm spending my Saturday morning making decorative, artisanal sex toys for my roommates and this is the thanks I get?"

I eye the water dripping from her fingers to the carpet. "I'm an ungrateful friend. Thank you."

"You're welcome. Jules said she's spending the weekend with She Who Will Not Be Named," Kat reminds me. "And I'm going home until tomorrow night. You going to be okay here alone?"

"Of course." The smile is in place before I'm sure I mean it, but my roommate seems satisfied.

I reach for my shoes. Having painted my toes a deep cabernet last night on a whim, the closed-toed pumps are a safer choice than the black-heeled sandals.

But the moody red matches my emotions today, so I choose the sandals.

The church parking lot is already full when I arrive. The truth that he was so well known and respected hits me.

Lancaster was a big deal in the academic world.

Kat asked me if I was going to be okay this weekend. But I'm not worried about me, I'm worried about the man who lost a father, after a lifetime of loss.

Inside, the pews are beginning to fill. I stand on my toes to search the crowd, there's no familiar dark head of messy hair. I need to see him. To make sure *he's* okay.

I find Sawyer pacing in the back room, his elegant suit at odds with his restlessness.

"Hi. You nervous?" I ask.

He turns, giving me a full view of his tailored suit, the jacket unbuttoned. When he spots me, his dark expression softens. "What are you doing here?"

"I told you I would be."

"I mean back here." He glances around the room.

This is a place for family. I'm not Lancaster's family. And as for what I am to the man in front of me...I have even less right to be here.

Instead of leaving, I square my shoulders and cross to him.

I brush a piece of lint off the lapel of his jacket. He flinches but doesn't move.

My fingers smooth down the front, slow and steady, and I tug the front closed, fastening the single button.

"Do you know what you're going to say?"

He nods to his chest, and I reach inside and pull out a sheet of notepaper with every inch filled, half of the words scribbled out with angry lines.

It's the closest I've come to knowing Sawyer's pain. He doesn't talk about it, but I feel it coming off the page in waves.

"Albert Lancaster was a monster," he says quietly. "He didn't give a shit about the people he was supposed to love."

"You're going to lead with that? Sounds like a real crowdpleaser."

Sawyer shoots me a chastising look. "A person can be an asshole their entire life, but when they die, they become a saint. You're not supposed to call them on their shit anymore. It's finally my chance to do it."

He turns away to pace the narrow room.

Sawyer might be impulsive and reckless, but he's not going to rip his heart open in front of all those people...is he?

He stops to rest his palms and head against the wall on the far side.

If someone came back, it would be odd to find the son of the man being celebrated today with one of his students.

Odd, but not wrong.

But when he bangs his head against the wallpaper, once, then again, and again, I can't stay still.

I cross to him and wrap my arms around him from behind. He stiffens under my touch, his body warm and hard.

"I'll stand by you if you want to tell that room the man he was to you." His jacket is rough against my lips as I speak. "But don't do it for them. Do it for you."

His rasping breath is painful to hear, and I hold him tighter as if I can fix this, can fix *him*.

"There were good moments," he murmurs at last. "When I figured out something he'd been trying to teach me for ages. When he let me help him on a new project. The fucked-up part is I remember them all, because they were so few and far between. It's not fair."

"No, but maybe we're built to remember the good times, even if they don't happen as much as we want. It's not a bug in our human code, it's a feature." Memories float to the surface of my mind. "I went to see him for the first time because I planned to drop engineering, starting with his class, and I wanted a signature. He asked me why I was leaving. I said I felt awkward around my classmates, geniuses like Royce and legacies like Adam. Even the girls didn't want to team up with me because they thought I was a liability."

Sawyer searches my face but doesn't say anything. I continue.

"Lancaster told me I didn't need anyone's permission to drop out, but I also didn't need permission to stay. That if I was waiting for another person to approve, I'd be waiting a long time." My lips curve at the corners. "If it wasn't for him, I would've dropped out."

"You're saying he was a better person than I give him credit for."

"We're all better and worse than anyone gives us credit for."

He grabs the back of my neck and leans in, his forehead pressing against mine.

I can't tell if it's a minute or an hour before a voice in the hall calls, "Sawyer?"

We spring apart.

"Are you ready?" the minister asks, appearing in the doorway.

Sawyer nods and I head down the hall and take a seat in one of the middle pews.

The minister says a few words before Sawyer takes his position at the front.

"I've been trying to put into words what Albert Lancaster was. Which is difficult because words were never currency in his house. If I had to choose ones I'd say he was extraordinary. Unexpected. Iconoclastic."

Gradually, my body relaxes as Sawyer runs through his father's achievements, ending on a story about what a genius the man was. How he believed in a better world than the one we existed in.

Even if he couldn't bring his son along for the ride.

Why didn't you? I want to ask Lancaster. Because the son in question is amazing. Raw, passionate, beautiful.

"You knew him well?" A man in the pew next to me leans over to whisper.

I nod slowly. "I think I did."

Now, all he's left behind are his work, and the man at the front.

I stare at the dark red toes peeking out from my sandals.

Sawyer wants me to experience the world. So did Lancaster. They went about it in different ways, Lancaster through patience and quiet belief, Sawyer through provocation.

After, Sawyer's swept up with other people, but when I get a reminder notification on my phone of a dinner reservation, I spot a text.

Unknown: Thank you.

Two simple words, freely given. My heart expands.

Liv: You were amazing. I'm going to meet my family for dinner before the basketball game.

When I shift into my car, I add one more.

Liv: Text me tonight.

***

"Too bad Adam couldn't join us for dinner," Mom says at halftime from our seats in the second row.

"He had to get ready with the team."

I'm only half watching, still thinking of Sawyer. Emma's next to me on her phone, Mom and Dad on my opposite side.

"He's very talented," my father says, nodding toward the bench.

"Would you say anything if he wasn't?" I tease.

"I don't need to hear this from you, Olivia. I've dealt with enough bullshit these past two weeks—"

"I was joking." They still think I'm with Adam. It helps that we've barely seen him, though he seems content enough to hold up the charade for now.

I re-cross my legs, and my mother stares at my toenails and black outfit.

"Please tell me you're not about to hit some gothic phase. This look is too austere."

"I was at a funeral," I remind her. Then turning to my dad, I say, "since you're here, I thought we could discuss my tuition for next semester."

"Olivia!" he hisses. "Not now. I want to have a nice evening with my family."

Impatience eats at my insides.

Earlier at dinner, he was approached by a stream of former classmates and faculty in town for homecoming, too.

He acted like he always had, but as they talked about real estate and markets and trips and policy, he seemed agitated.

My phone buzzes.

Unknown: I'm at the game. Where are you?

The hairs on my arms lift in awareness.

When I look up, my gaze locks with Sawyer's. He's at the end of the row, and heading this way.

It's one thing for my home life and what I'm experiencing with my professor to clash in my head. Having them clash in reality isn't only confusing, it's dangerous.

He stops in front of us. He's changed since the funeral, now wearing dark jeans and a white shirt rolled up to his elbows and open at the collar.

"Professor Redmond. Mom and Dad, this is my engineering professor. Adam's and mine," I amend.

They shake hands, my mother looking like she can't decide whether to stare at Sawyer's muscled forearms or turn her nose up at his casual clothes.

Emma nudges me. *Your professor? OMG*, she mouths.

"Mr. and Mrs. Barclay. You must be proud of Olivia. She's one of the most hardworking students in my class." I turn to stare at Sawyer, warmth spreading over me as he continues. "Her team's submission has a legitimate chance at regionals at the end of the month."

A bewildered look crosses between my parents. "Her what?"

"This must be Adam's project," Mom decides. "Olivia, I didn't realize you were participating."

Sawyer frowns, looking between us.

Let it go.

I'll tell my parents, but not until I can get tuition for next semester. They'll say I need to find the right partner, Adam or someone like him, and the Stars project is only a distraction.

Because there's no way I could secure the kind of future they want for me, *expect* for me, myself.

"Could I have a word?" My professor's gaze is firmly on me. I follow him around behind the bleachers.

He pins me to them, his breath hot on my face. "Care to fill me in?"

"They don't know about Stars. Engineering was never a major they wanted for me, it was one they permitted because it was a way to stay close to Adam." He blinks, incredulous. "I play along because I have to, not because I want to. You wouldn't understand."

"Try me."

I lift my chin. "I'm doing this for my sister."

"So she can learn that the way to get ahead is by bending to other people?"

"No! I want her to be free. Who do you think pays for my school? My life? And Emma's, too? And if that wasn't enough, my dad's company is having problems. I don't know how bad they are, but it's worse than they're letting on. If I don't keep up appearances…I could lose everything."

Sawyer's chest rises and falls, agitated. "But you've already lost. If you try to appease them, you lose yourself. You want to be a big girl? That doesn't come from dancing on a pole or blowing your professor in a dark hallway."

I wrench out of his grip. "Easy for you to say! You can go wherever you want and say whatever you want, because you aren't responsible for anyone else. You're an island."

I turn away, still fuming.

When I return to my parents, my father is chatting with another couple. "Olivia, I have some former classmates for you to meet."

"It's so kind of you to come all this way with your family to support your boyfriend this weekend," the woman says warmly, nodding to the bench where Adam sits in a huddle with his teammates.

I look between them and my parents. "I go to Russell. This is my school, too." My toes clench in my shoes. "And it's not Adam's engineering team," I say to my parents. "It's mine. I'm the team lead, and it's a prestigious competition."

I grab my things and bolt for the doors right as the game resumes.

15

OLIVIA

"Where do you think you're going?" a familiar voice rasps in the dark when I reach the sidewalk outside.

"Home."

My heels click on the concrete path as I stalk away from the athletic center. Sawyer follows a few paces behind.

"Maybe I don't know your life," he calls. "But I saw you with them tonight, saw the way you looked as if all you wanted was to get out of there...I wanted to take care of you."

His rough voice is at odds with the gentleness of his words.

My chest tightens. "I appreciate the sentiment. But like I told you, I'm going back to my dorm. You can't come. Even if..."

"If what?"

If I wanted you to.

Even with Kat and Jules gone for the weekend, it's too risky for a faculty member to be seen near my dorm room.

When we get near the doors of my building, I tense up. There are half a dozen students in the foyer, plus more with parents strolling outside. Some are taking pictures in front of the elm trees that ring the building.

It's dark out here, but inside, the lights are bright.

"Which one's you?" Sawyer asks under his breath.

I peer around the side of the building, nodding to the second-floor balcony. "Third one from the end. That's our living room."

He looks around, his gaze landing on the trees outside. "Meet you up there."

"What? How?"

But he tosses me a grin and makes me go inside.

I run up the stairs and burst into the apartment, dragging open the patio door.

"Oh my God. You're insane! Did anyone see you?"

He's already hauling himself over the wall of our balcony, grunting with exertion.

"Nope. It's dark, and I've done this before. It's been a few years," he admits at my incredulous look. "Come on. Did you eat dinner with your parents?"

"Kind of." I mostly pushed the food around my plate.

"I'll make you my specialty."

He follows me inside and searches through our cupboards. "How are you alive?"

"Knowledge sustains me."

I love having him in my space. He's big and male and surreal, and I soak in the sight of him moving around our kitchen like a pirate, his long hair tousled and the white shirt untucked on one side from climbing the tree.

"You've been alive, what, three decades and this is your specialty?" I ask when he pushes a PB&J sandwich and a glass full of ice water over.

"No. But it's the best I could do under the circumstances."

I reach for the sandwich but he holds out a hand to stop me.

"Wait."

He grabs the knife and cuts off the crusts. My heart does a little flip.

"I can't believe you just did that."

"Looked like you needed it."

How does he see me? And want to take care of me?

I take a bite, chewing while he watches as if I might spit it out.

"That's good."

"You bet your ass it is." He grins and turns to set the knife in the sink, but freezes.

"What's wrong?"

Sawyer reaches for something in the sink, turning and holding up the enormous clay "sculpture" Kat made earlier.

"Is this..."

I choke on the sandwich, coughing until it's gone down the right way. Then I grin. "Is this what?"

"When you called me that night, is this the toy you used?"

I die.

I'm face-first on the counter, my shoulders shaking with laughter.

"It's Kat's," I say when I can breathe again, wiping the tears from my eyes. "She calls them her art. She says it's functional but given the dimensions, my guess is it's more...decorative."

"I see." He sets the thing on the counter as if it might leap up and bite him.

"Are you intimidated?"

"No."

"Really?"

He leans in and brushes the corner of my mouth, finding a bit of peanut butter. Then sucks it off his finger in a way that makes my stomach flutter. "Not even a little. What else did you want to do tonight?"

God, there are so many ways I'd like to spend an evening with him.

"One thing springs to mind."

An hour later we're sitting across from one another. Sawyer drums his fingers on the table before sneaking a brick out of the tower.

"It's going to fall."

"It is not."

The bricks wobble, and I suck in a delighted breath.

But he slides the brick out and the tower remains upright.

"Hah!" he exclaims. "Your move."

I screw up my face and start poking at wooden pieces to see if any are free.

They're all gone.

I reach for one on a side that's more securely anchored. Then close my eyes and slide it carefully...

The tower stays standing.

"Voodoo magic," he declares.

"Physics," I correct, solemn. "The best of all the sciences."

His lips twitch. "Your sister is lucky to have you."

"Sometimes I'm not sure." The change of subject makes me lean back on my hands.

"I would've killed for an older brother or sister. I might've turned out better if I had one."

My gaze drags over his body, lingering on his face. "You turned out fine to me," I say softly.

He smiles. "She looks a lot like you."

"One of Adam's friends called her Olivia The Second when she started at our high school, promising he'd to get in her pants by winter break. I told him if he touched her I'd cut off his balls with a nail file." I arch a brow. "So don't get any ideas."

He grabs the table, hard enough the tower comes crashing down. "I'm not a cradle robber."

Can nobody take a joke tonight?

He takes our glasses to the kitchen while I collect the JENGA pieces, one at a time.

"I just...don't want you thinking this is something I do," he says at last.

"This? Playing JENGA with younger women?"

"Exactly." There's a hint of teasing in his voice, but underneath, he's serious.

When he returns, I stand, folding my arms. "Right. And why would I think that?"

His gaze searches mine. "Because I'm used to people thinking the worst of me."

The low confession is startlingly raw. To the world, he's capable, even arrogant, flaunting the rules at every turn.

But he has reasons to be that way. Every scar he carries was a gaping wound he tended, healed until it was almost invisible.

I want to kiss him so badly.

Sawyer steps closer, tugging out my ponytail and pushing his fingers through my hair. It feels so good, and I barely resist the urge to moan.

He twists a strand around his finger. "You always had it long?"

"Since I was six. I was so proud I grew it past my shoulders. My mom sent me to school with it in braids, but I took it out because I liked the feel of it down. Then a boy at school came up behind me and stuck gum in the ends. When my mother found out, she said it was my fault and cut it all off."

"The gum."

I shake my head. "My hair. She used kitchen scissors, she was so mad. Had to call a stylist to come to our house and try to turn it into a bob after, but it was barely long enough for that. But"

—I suck in a breath—"we all have our shit, right? Better she take it out on me than on Emma."

I lift my gaze to find Sawyer watching me. "She has a problem with a single hair on your head ever again, you send her to me."

Warmth spreads through my chest at his fierce protectiveness. I don't know what I did to earn it, but I don't ever want to lose it.

He does a double take at the tidy rows of blocks on the table. "You even store your JENGA set perfectly. You are a nerd."

He grabs me, tossing me over his shoulder.

I gasp, grabbing onto his waist for balance. "You're the one with post-grad degrees."

He drops me on the couch, and I bounce, breathless. He shifts over me, holding himself up on his elbows.

He's fun, this version of my professor. I didn't expect the playfulness, but damn, it's addictive.

"Did you ever play games with your dad?" I ask. Not an epic conversational segue, but it's all I can come up with given how close he is.

"He kept a Go set in his office at home." Sawyer tucks a piece of hair behind my ear. "I hated it, he was better than me."

"Better than me, too. There's a set in his office at the department," I remind him, thinking of the thousands-year-old strategy game displayed on the shelf behind Lancaster's desk.

He cocks his head. "You played him?"

"Once or twice." I reach up to touch his face, afraid of breaking this spell between us. "You want to talk about what happened today?"

He's warm under my hand, and when my thumb brushes up his jaw, he shudders. "No."

He reaches for me, grabbing my face between his palms.

Sawyer kisses me with hunger. His firm lips rub across mine, coaxing mine apart.

He's hard and commanding. A brick wall with an agenda.

When his tongue sneaks inside my mouth, I arch against him. Need streaks through my body, starting at the places we're touching and echoing deep in my stomach, my breasts, between my thighs.

But the connection between us is more than that. It's the understanding, the feeling of being trapped expecting more from someone we trusted but knowing we can't complain.

His touch moves downward, squeezing my breasts, smoothing over my waist. I feel him dig his fingers, straining my panties tight across my skin through the dress.

I start to reach for them when he pulls back an inch.

"Leave them on."

He stands and lifts me in his arms, backing me toward a doorway.

I blink my eyes open. "Not my room."

Laughing, he steers us toward one of the other two, slamming the door behind us with a finality that vibrates through me.

Sawyer doesn't look around, as if the world doesn't matter.

He sets me on the edge of my desk, shoving back the chair.

"You didn't want me to leave them on in your office," I pant.

"My father's office."

"It's yours now."

My hands find his shirt, unbuttoning all the way down without tearing my mouth from his.

"You're mine now."

He lets me off the desk long enough to unzip my dress and tug it over my head. When it's on the floor, he takes me in, gaze ravenous.

I've never felt as good as when Sawyer looks at me.

"The other night on the phone...that was unreal."

He shoves down the cup of my black bra and drops his head to my hardened nipple, sucking.

My fingers twist in his hair, tugging him closer. "I wish you could've gotten off too."

"I did."

He rubs his fingers against me through my panties. I'm already beyond wet.

"I haven't been able to stop thinking about it," I admit, the words spilling out now.

"What do you think about?"

Every breath is a futile attempt to get enough oxygen to my lungs. I'm overwhelmed by him, by the way he wants me. I've never known there was a desire this strong.

"Your face between my thighs."

I suck at asking for what I want, especially when it's something I've been told I shouldn't ask for. But with him, it feels easy. Natural.

"I think about that, too. Especially since it's not something you've had much experience with." His eyes darken.

I hope he doesn't think I'm entirely naïve.

"Do you trust me, Cherry Bomb?"

"Yes."

When he pulls my thong to the side, I can't think anymore.

Sawyer shifts down my body. I'm not scared, only excited.

I want to like this, but I want him to like it, too. Is that even possible?

"So fucking gorgeous." He presses my thighs further apart, as if admiring one of the paintings hanging in my parents' living room.

A flush crawls up my cheeks. I try to close my legs an inch, but he holds them wide.

I'm completely exposed and vulnerable. When he tugs my hips forward, my hands brace behind me for balance.

His gaze flicks up to meet mine for a heartbeat, and the heat and intensity in it shakes me to the core.

He lifts two fingers to my lips. The light pressure coaxes me to open and I take both in my mouth. The sudden invasion is strange, but I like having him in me this way. My tongue sneaks forward on instinct, wrapping around him, exploring him.

When he pulls his hand back, there's a little pop from me trying to keep him inside.

"Good girl. Not that we're going to need it," he murmurs as he lowers his hand.

I swallow. There's suddenly way too much saliva in my mouth.

He strokes me where I'm aching, two wet fingers touching me at once, and the world explodes.

He feels so good. Everything feels so good when he's stroking me, rubbing little circles that make my core tingle and my fingers dig into his neck.

He shifts closer, his warm breath landing where I'm bare and making me tremble.

Yes.

Yes, please.

I need...

His tongue brushes me, sweeping a long path up that ends with a stroke over my clit.

But then he pulls back.

"Tell me how you like it." His breath is hot against my skin, his gaze hungry as he looks up at me through dark lashes.

"What?"

"You've had enough people telling you what you want tonight. So tell me what feels good. Talk to me."

The throbbing need in my core turns into a full-body ache.

I want you, looking at me exactly like this. Forever.

The numbers on my bedside clock change, the soft glow from the table lamp familiar.

There's no hurry.

Only the most beautiful man I've ever seen, on his knees in front of me.

"I want your mouth on me. I want to feel your tongue so deep, it's like I'm burning up from the inside out."

Sawyer's jaw clenches as if he's never heard anything sexier in his life.

My grip finds his hair and guides him back between my thighs. This time, I'm ready. At least, I think I am, until his tongue does that sweeping thing again.

"Yeah," I sigh. "Right there..."

This time the pleasure comes in a wave, a long, endless swell. The edge comes after, quieter but every bit as insistent.

I fall back, my head touching the wall.

Fuck, his mouth.

His smug, beautiful, sweet, filthy mouth.

There's a fire starting in my core.

I arch against his tongue.

"Sawyer."

My moan rips through the stillness of the room, and he stiffens. As if me using his given name is a reminder of how fucking wrong this is.

"Say it again." His mouth vibrates against me, and all the tension releases in a wave.

"Sawyer. Dammit, Sawyer—"

I'm coming.

My fingers twist in his hair, yanking as if I can control him or me or this.

But I'm so lost and for once, I don't even care.

Because even though I'm out of control, one reverberation of pleasure crashing into the next, I don't *feel* lost. I feel found.

When I recover enough to sit up, he shoots me a dark grin. Then he lifts me and sets me on the center of the bed.

"Like your toes," he says, grabbing for one.

I grin as I twist away. "Thanks."

I reach back to unfasten my bra, still awkwardly underneath my breasts, and toss it off the side of the bed.

Sawyer groans. "You just keep getting better."

"That's all it takes to bring the great Sawyer Redmond to his knees? Tits?"

"If they're yours, yes."

He shifts over me, taking my breasts in his rough palms. His mouth descends, nibbling and licking and sucking every inch of me until I'm writhing on the bed.

I can feel his hardness against my leg, the impossible length and girth of him.

Not so different from Kat's "art" in dimensions, in fact. But it's attached to a living, breathing man who turns me inside out.

"You're stunning, Olivia," he murmurs in my ear. "I need all of you."

Sawyer rears back and reaches for his belt,

unfastening it with steady hands. Then the button on his pants and the zipper.

Without breaking my gaze, he stands next to the bed and drags his pants off.

His erection stretches the cotton of his boxer briefs, and my pulse thuds in my back.

In my peripheral vision, a photoboard on my bedside table has me closing my eyes.

I've only slept with one other person. Even though I want this, so badly, it feels as if so much has changed in such a short time.

"Can we...I need a minute."

His face slackens in confusion. "Yeah."

I drop back onto my bed, aroused and embarrassed at once. "I'm sorry. I—"

"Don't apologize. I have no expectations."

The bed sinks next to me, and I blink my eyes open to see him lying on his side, concerned.

I run a finger along his collarbone. "What's this dent?"

"Broke it as a kid. Fell off the roof."

"You're joking."

A head shake. "Hurt like hell."

"You could've come up with a good story." I play with his hair. "Motocross. Threesome gone wrong."

He shifts over me, setting an elbow on either

side of my head. "I don't want to make things up. Not with you."

I can't feel the wrongness of this moment anymore. All I feel is right here with him, so fucking right. "I'm ready."

But when I reach for the fabric of his underwear, he shifts away, pulling me down the bed and spreading my thighs.

"What are you doing?"

"Making you come again."

"We're not going to...?"

"We have a lot of missed pleasure to make up for. Besides, if you're screaming my name, I don't much care how we're doing it."

This time, it's even hotter, because I'm more relaxed.

My hands grab his hair, his back, his ass. I touch him anywhere I want and he finger fucks me with utter entitlement.

"Tell me when you're going to come."

"Soon."

"How soon?"

I groan, sink my teeth into his neck. "Fucking soon, asshole."

He laughs and three pumps later, I'm clenching around him, pleasure ripping through me.

"It's Professor Redmond," he says, swatting my ass lightly when I recover.

"But I like calling you Sawyer."

His expression is conflicted. "I like hearing it."

But only here, he might as well say.

This isn't the real world, it's a fantasy.

For now, I'll enjoy it.

This time when his touch returns, it's a slow stroke that makes me curl up off the bed. But he holds me down with an arm over my stomach.

I do come again, and it's not an explosion, it's a slip. My center of gravity being yanked out from under me, a breathless tumble down, down, down.

Nothing feels as right as coming apart in his arms.

When I blink my heavy eyes open, Sawyer's pulling on his pants. I scramble up to sitting.

"Where are you going?"

"I can't stay the night." His hands still on the button of his jeans. "Olivia..."

My throat tightens, because *shit*. I don't want him to leave.

But of course he can't stay. It's a student dorm. It was reckless enough to come here in the dark, but walking out Sunday morning...he might as well carry a flashing sign saying, "I'm fucking a student, ask me how."

"Please." The word surprises us both. "I can sneak you out. Hell, you can stay all day. We'll lie in bed and eat peanut butter sandwiches, and…"

He shoves his hair out of his face to meet my eyes. Whatever he sees there has his shoulders caving.

He jerks his head and I shift back to make room. Then, jeans still on, he crawls under the covers and tugs me back against his chest.

As I fall asleep in his arms, I think this might be even better than the sex.

16

OLIVIA

I wake up to empty sheets that smell like Sawyer.

The light streaming in around the curtains says it's morning, but all I can think about is being wrapped in strong arms all night long.

Did he leave without saying goodbye? Disappointment has my heart sinking until I glance over to the nightstand and see his watch.

My lips curve.

He's still here.

The sound of a door slamming followed by female laughter drifts through the apartment.

What the...

I slide out of bed, grab a robe, and trip across the room to the half-open door.

Kat and Jules are in the foyer, kicking off their shoes.

"Thought you guys were gone for the weekend," I manage, rubbing the sleep from my eyes.

"We came back early." Jules hangs up her denim jacket, then cuts a look at the bathroom. "If you're not in there…"

The shower's on.

Shit.

We all turn to look at the same time.

"You brought Adam home?" Jules demands.

"I'm going to kick his…" Kat trails off as the water cuts out. Her sunglasses are still on her face and I can't make out her expression.

I hold my breath for five seconds.

Ten.

The door opens.

Sawyer walks out in a towel.

I can't breathe, or look at anyone.

It's not that bad. Not that bad. Not that…

He pulls up when he sees my roomies.

"Um. Professor…Sawyer. This is Kat. And Jules." I wave a hand between them. No one says anything. "Do you want a coffee? Or pants?"

Kat pulls her sunglasses down her nose. "Don't put clothes on for our sake."

Sawyer shoves a hand through his hair and

mine isn't the only gaze that drags down his gorgeous body.

But his attention is squarely on me, his beautiful mouth pursed. "Yes to clothes. Rain check on coffee. Excuse us."

He grabs me by the tie on my robe and tugs me back to my room.

"What just happened?" Jules asks Kat before Sawyer slams the door.

"Those are my roommates," I blurt as Sawyer backs me against it. "I didn't know they'd be coming back."

His hair drips onto the floor, then onto the skin exposed by my robe when he's close enough.

Why can't I stop staring at his body?

"You're in so much trouble." He traces the necklace I forgot to take off last night, pressing the diamond pendant at the center against my collarbone.

"They won't tell."

"Uh-huh."

He tugs at the tie on my robe.

Before he can open it, Sawyer's phone buzzes on my desk.

"You need to get it?" I whisper when he doesn't move.

"No. But I need to leave." He crosses to grab

the phone. "Daniel's helping me fix up the house, and the prick won't let me pay him. Told him I'd watch Andy today."

"Well, aren't you Mr. Adorable." Now that I can breathe, I can't resist teasing him.

He catches sight of my lazy grin. "I answer to 'Professor Redmond.' Or, where you're concerned, 'Dear God Sawyer Yes' will also suffice."

I laugh, even though his words make me hot all over again. "Nah, I'm going to change your name in my phone. You're 'Mr. Adorable' from here on out."

The next second I'm back against the door, his hands in my robe and his mouth bruising mine.

I reach for the knot in his towel, ready to demolish it and anything else that comes between us.

Sawyer pulls back with a groan, pressing his forehead to mine. "You're going to ruin me."

"I'm not trying to."

"That's why it's working."

His lips brush my forehead and when he turns away, I could pout. I want him to stay here all morning.

He drops the towel, tossing it on the back of my desk chair.

My heart stops beating.

He's incredible, his body still damp from his shower. His defined chest and abs leading into a fine line of dark hair that trails down between his legs. And between those legs, he's long and thick even half hard from our kiss.

Oh my God.

Naked, he looks even bigger than at Fall Ball.

Does a woman need to work up to that?

Before I can ask, he's tugging on his briefs and pants.

I adjust my robe and get his shirt, passing it to him. He takes it, looks at the photos around my mirror as he shrugs into the shirt.

"This is you dancing?" He points to a picture from an old competition.

"Pointe shoes were my life." It's weird having Sawyer see pieces of my past, but good weird, not bad weird. He doesn't look away as his capable hands fasten the buttons on his shirt.

He tucks his phone into a pocket with a smile. "I'd like to see you dance."

"Theresa said I could use the studio after classes let out and the competition team is done practicing. But that's usually late, and I have to get up for early class. Plus, the extra lab time for Stars."

"Tell me you're not working on the project

today." He steps close, winding a piece of my hair around his fingers.

"Yeah, after I meet Emma for a bit. Madison will point it out if I'm slacking."

"I can't picture you slacking." He nods to my bookshelf, half full of textbooks. "You know why I made you team lead?"

"Because I jumped you in a utility closet?" I bite my lip and he chuckles.

"Because you don't give up." He bends toward me and brushes his lips across my cheek.

"You're late," calls my sister over the white picket fence surrounding the patio at Some Like It Hot.

I turn into the café's walkway and drop into the seat across from her. "By five minutes."

Of the six tables out front, three are occupied. The mad rush on cinnamon buns seems to be over.

"But you're never late." My little sister folds her arms, eyes bright.

"Things change."

A waitress comes out to greet us. I order a coffee and croissant and Emma opts for a tea as we watch people pass on the cute street.

"How's cheerleading going?" I ask.

"Savage. Our director came back from camp this summer with crazy new ideas. She's mostly taking them out on the tumblers." Emma holds out her arm, displaying a huge bruise.

"Ouch."

"It's okay. I'm tough. You know that, right?"

"Of course I know that." I lean in, brushing her hair back behind her shoulder. "Is that bruise from cheerleading too?" I point to her neck and she grins.

"Nope. I have a fan of my own. I got to ride a motorcycle." She pulls out her phone, showing me a picture of a boy with dark hair and mischievous eyes straddling a huge bike. "He's twenty-two."

Our drinks and my pastry arrive, and I rip off a piece of croissant.

"He looks kind of tough, Ems."

"It's not like...if you were dating that professor guy who showed up last night. He must be at least thirty?"

"Not 'at least.'" I take an extra-large gulp of coffee, burning my mouth. "And it's not the age that matters. It's how you connect with another person. You could connect with someone twice your age."

"Exactly. We have that kind of connection! I

can't stop thinking about him. I want to be around him all the time."

Damn if I don't know what that feels like.

I can't breathe when Sawyer's around. Every second I'm with him leaves me wanting more. I love every time he shows me one of his scars, not only the ones on his body but on his soul, because he's used to growling at anyone who gets near.

I love the way he looks at me, as if I'm fascinating and challenging and enough, even when I feel like none of those things.

I love that his laugh makes me tingle, that his touch makes me weak, that his confidence makes me strong.

A bicycle flies by the patio, close enough I feel the breeze on my arms.

"You're still judging me, I can feel it. Don't be like Mom," Emma says.

I straighten. "I'm not like Mom. I'm trying to protect you from Mom."

"I don't need your protection. Whatever you're doing to handle them, don't do it for me."

I want to say, *but you don't know what's happening.*

My dad's car pulls up, parking along the curb.

"How mad are Mom and Dad that I bailed last night?" I murmur.

"On a scale of one to that time I dyed my hair purple right before piano recital?" Emma scrunches up her face. "Twenty."

I'm glad I stood up for myself, but now in the light of day, I need to deal with the fallout.

I tense as my parents shift out.

"I hope you're feeling better after last night," Dad starts as he stops in front of the patio.

There's genuine concern on his face. My mother's...I can't tell from behind her Prada sunglasses.

"I am." *Thanks to Sawyer.* "I'm sorry for leaving abruptly."

Mom cuts in. "And not cheering for Adam? I'm sure that's not how his future fiancée should behave."

My dad clears his throat. "Did you girls pay yet? I'll get the check."

Emma waves him inside, and follows. "I'm going to use the bathroom."

Once they've gone, I watch as Mom takes the plate with the rest of my croissant and sets it at the edge of the table.

"First, it was an exhibition game. And second..." I take a deep breath. "Adam and I broke up. He didn't want me."

"He said that." Mom's face pales.

"He *showed* me," I say, thinking of the girls he slept with. "I get that you were invested in this, but I won't tie myself to someone who doesn't want to be with me."

"What's the alternative? Being alone, wasting yourself?"

I think of the man I spent last night with.

Not alone. Not wasted.

"Some things are more important than what you want," she goes on, her penciled brows lowering. "The security you enjoy pays for what you eat, what you wear, even your precious school."

"And we might be losing it anyway." I grab her wrist above the Cartier bangle. "I'm sure what's happening with Dad's company scares you. It scares me, too. But I can't keep trying to be someone I'm not." The backs of my eyes burn. "On some level, you must understand that."

For a moment, I swear she's going to nod.

But her mouth only tightens, her attention shifting to the remainder of my croissant as she rises from her seat. "Just because you've quit dance doesn't mean you should stop caring about your figure."

17

OLIVIA

"Hoes Over Brews, take two."

Kat and Jules clink their beer glasses against mine at the bar Sunday night.

"I still haven't heard why you got home early," I point out.

"I crashed at this guy's place, but woke up to him doing laundry." Kat sways her hips to the music, eyeing up the dart board.

"That's a bad thing?" Jules teases.

"In the middle of the night. I slipped out of bed to find him in the laundry room down the hall, get this—*rolling* his underwear."

Kat tosses the dart, which thuds into the cork an inch from the bullseye.

"Wait, I thought you were going home to see family?" I frown.

"Did that. But I ran into someone I used to hook up with in high school at the grocery store. I have the attention span of a goldfish," she finishes when I laugh.

"Research shows the average human attention span has dropped from twelve to eight seconds. A goldfish's attention span is about nine seconds."

"There you go." The next dart lands right in the bullseye.

"Did you have any doctor's appointments?" I ask.

"No. I'll go at winter break. I'm fine," she sighs at my look, grabbing me by the shoulders.

"We just want your ass healthy," Jules prods.

Kat turns toward her. "What about your ass, hmm?"

"There's nothing wrong with my ass."

"Exactly. That's why I want what's best for you, and She Who Will Not—"

"She has a name. It's Tess."

"And she doesn't deserve you."

"I want her anyway." Jules reaches for her beer.

Kat's gaze meets mine.

The next instant we descend on Jules, a group hug without warning.

"Okay, enough!" she protests, laughing.

"How's little sis?" Kat asks me. "And your parents?"

"Emma's good. My parents are having money problems, but they won't talk about it."

"What did they say when you told them about Adam?"

"My mom freaked. She's not in denial about me and Adam, but afterward, she gave me this look of total disdain. As if she didn't recognize me."

"Well at least now everything's out in the open," Jules says.

The subject of tuition is nowhere near resolved, but I don't want to dump that at their feet now.

Kat cocks her head. "What about the part where you're fucking your professor?"

The beer in my glass sloshes against the side as I grab her arm. "A little louder for the people in the back."

She lowers her voice. "Unless you're going to claim the man chained to your bed all night isn't the one grading your midterms."

I snatch the dart from Kat's fingers. "He wasn't chained to my bed. We played JENGA. Things escalated."

"As they do." Jules shifts back in her seat.

"You just decided fuck it, let's be together on campus at a dorm?" Kat asks.

I line up my shot, visualizing the dart hitting the target. When I toss it after the first two of Kat's, it misses by inches.

"It was his idea more than mine."

"And how was it?"

I retrieve the darts from the board, a shiver coursing through me. "Insanely good. Like...I didn't know it could feel that good kind of good."

Kat hollers and I roll my eyes.

"I know I only broke up with Adam a few weeks ago, but I never felt this way with him. It's like whenever Sawyer's close, the world is bigger and more full of possibility. As if every dark moment suddenly has a silver lining."

"Awww." Kat bats her lashes. "And it has nothing to do with the fact that he's built like a god and makes you want to confess all your sins and be punished for them one at a time?"

"Nothing," I maintain, grinning.

Jules' expression is concerned. "What happens when he runs into students? You could get in big trouble. Both of you."

I reach for my drink, but it's already empty.

He texted me a picture of Andy feeding the fish this afternoon. It melted my heart, but there was none of the usual sexy dig accompanying it, or since.

It's only been a day, but I expected Sawyer to at least be teasing me about how many times I moaned his name last night.

Unless he's angry about us getting caught.

He risked everything to spend the night with me. I want him more than ever. Every second of today, I was imagining him touching me again.

"I don't know," I admit.

An attractive couple a few years older cuts between us and the dart board on the way to the bar, him grabbing her ass and her dragging his mouth up to hers.

We can't ever do that, have that, be that. Even our attraction has to be in secret.

The fact that our relationship is completely illicit has always been thrilling, but for the first time, it feels like I'm missing out.

18

SAWYER

"Oof!" Betty trips reaching for the automatic door button outside the engineering building Monday morning.

I run to catch her by her blue football jersey—celebrating the home team's win yesterday, no doubt.

"What are you doing with all those?" I nod to the stack of files on a cart.

"The dean wanted them for meetings today."

"They're not digital?"

She screws up her face. "Most are, but we're behind on updating historical files. The dean cut the summer student position that used to help me with tasks like this."

Typical.

I grab the cart from her and wave to the door.

"You're here early," she says. "The only students around are still drunk from Homecoming."

I laugh. "Need to prep for classes. I had less time on the weekend than I expected."

"Your father's service was beautiful, Sawyer. I hope you got some time to unwind after."

Unwind. That's one word for it.

I followed Olivia home and spent the entire night with her, plus a good part of the next morning.

It was hot, but even more than that, I enjoyed her company.

I didn't plan on any of it, especially feeling the way I felt with her.

Relaxed.

Whole.

At peace.

When you've gone without, it's hard to know what enough looks like. But with Olivia, the restlessness I've always felt goes quiet.

I told her she isn't perfect, but I was wrong. Her perfection is in her ability to open up despite everything she carries on her narrow shoulders, and the way she listens without judgment. It was all I could do not to grab her parents and shake them until they understood what an unbelievable woman they raised and how much she just wants someone to see her for who she is, not some fake, compliant creature.

Betty and I pull up next to the elevator where she stabs at a button.

Nothing happens. No light on the panel, no whooshing of pulley systems.

"Dammit. Not working," she mutters.

"How important is this meeting?"

"It's with the Board of Governors." She makes a face. "Alumni support is down at the moment. It's part of the reason the department finances are stretched."

"I'm offended the dean didn't come to ask me personally."

"He wouldn't ask you if you were the last rich graduate on earth." Betty's laugh fades as she eyes up the boxes. "I need to get these upstairs. Guess we'll take them one box at a time."

She reaches for the top box on the stack but I wave her off. "Give me five minutes."

I toss her a grin before running up to my office.

Up there, I search through the closet for some supplies.

It takes no time to rig up a system that runs through a pulley, attached to the top of my window frame, with bungee cords to hold each box.

I lean out the window. "Loop the cord around the box."

She does it, shaking her head.

When all five boxes are inside, I meet Betty at her desk.

"Well that was the high point of today," she says, gleeful. "I was starting to wonder if you'd left that smile in New York."

Before I can process that, she continues.

"The dean is starting to try and poach donors from other departments. Livvy Barclay's father is top on the list."

Protectiveness rises up. I don't want him anywhere near Olivia or her family, especially given their money problems. It'll only stress her out more.

Of course, I'm doing a terrible job of protecting her so far—I stayed in her damned apartment.

On campus.

Where anyone could've discovered us, and hell, her roommates did.

"Don't worry about department politics," Betty says, misinterpreting my concern. "We're all human, Sawyer. He's trying to do his job like you're trying to do yours."

When I reach my office, I pull out a pen from

my bag and the materials for the Stars competition.

Thumbing through the pages of the forms, I spot a logo on one corner.

Regionals are in two more weeks. I can use that to pull the dean's attention to another area that matters to the school: publicity.

"How's life as an academic?" a crisp voice answers when I call.

"Idyllic, Tate. You should try it."

My former rival chuckles. "Never would've thought five years ago that we'd be going into business together."

"We should be halfway to a market capitalization of five hundred million by now."

"Don't pretend it's my fault we're not."

I turn the pen in my fingers, noticing the logo from my former company wrapped around the barrel. When I toss it in the garbage, there's a giant blob of ink on the inside of my finger.

"I'm overseeing RU's submission to the Stars engineering competition." I reach for a tissue, wiping my hands.

"Small world. Would you believe we're a sponsor?"

"That's why I'm calling. I want you to email our dean. Tell him you're excited about Russell's submission."

"Why?"

"Politics. Below your paygrade."

"I won't even have to lie. This contest is big, Sawyer. Having a team do well is good exposure for our future endeavors. And speaking of our plans, there's a big conference in L.A. this winter. Lots of industry contacts. I figured we could both go."

He tells me the dates, and that it's a week long.

"I have to teach, Tate."

"You'll miss, what, two classes? Three? Get a grad student to cover."

It's not impossible, and I did have someone cover for me the time I watched Andy for Daniel.

"I'll think about it."

"You're more serious about this professor thing than I gave you credit for. I'm impressed."

I can't tell Tate that it's not my class I don't want to leave for a week.

It's *her.*

When we hang up, I stare at the ink that won't come off.

I should walk away from Olivia Barclay. Not only because we were nearly caught, but for reasons I've been ignoring since I came to Russell.

Ones I can barely face myself, not to mention

admit to her.

I grab one of the Go pieces off the set on the shelf and hurl it across the room. It hits the plaster with a sharp "plink" and drops to the carpet.

A knock has me looking toward the door to see Olivia, fresh-faced and smiling.

She's wearing a sweater and dark jeans tight enough I bet she'd make that breathy sound I like if I stuck both my hands in her back pockets at once.

I resist the urge to run a hand through my hair to make sure it's not standing up.

The last time we were together, we were naked—or practically—but the sounds from the hallway remind me this is a different time and place.

Here, I'm a professor. She's a student.

Doesn't stop my abs from tightening in anticipation.

You're so fucked for her.

"What's that?" I nod to the colorful gift bag, complete with ribbons.

She pushes the door mostly closed before setting the bag on my desk.

I tug out the frothy sheets of tissue arranged in the top, chuckling when I see what's inside.

"JENGA."

"I bought it for you in town. Figured it was more you than the Go set." Olivia bends to pick up the piece from the carpet, her mouth twitching. "Looks like I was right."

Her consideration shouldn't suck all the air from the room, but it does. Or maybe it's the way she's looking at me, hopeful and earnest.

"Thank you."

I take the Go game and drop it into a file drawer. Olivia sets her bag on the guest chair and sets the JENGA game up on the corner of my desk.

"There. Now you can play with anyone who comes in." She smiles, adjusting the edges of the stacked blocks.

"I only want to play with you."

Her gaze lifts to mine.

She needs to stop looking at me as if I'm the inventor of every good thing in the world.

I can help her claim her power, but I'm not a man she can rely on. The call with Tate reminded me of that.

But I missed her since Saturday, dammit.

She reaches for an inside block near the base of the tower and slides it out, centering it on top. Before letting go, she changes her mind and slides it to one edge—a riskier move more likely to unbalance the entire structure.

"Are you trying to build a tower or bring one down?"

Vulnerability flickers across her face as she cocks her head, making the diamond around her neck sparkle in the light from the window. "I haven't decided."

That's the problem.

This started off as a reckless indulgence. I'm the king of those, I can spot them a mile away. And if it was only me she'd be bringing down, maybe I would risk it.

But it's her future, too. What we're doing could be adding to her challenges instead of helping them.

When this thing between us runs its course, I want her to be better off, not worse.

I take my block from the base, setting it to offset and balance hers. "We need to qualify a project in two weeks at regionals. A colleague I'm going into business with is one of the sponsors of the competition. I'd like the team to walk me through a working demo next week."

"Sure." She tucks a piece of hair behind her ear, waiting for me to say more.

Like that I keep thinking about how her lower lip trembles when she comes. Or that I could bury my face in her throat, her hair, for hours just breathing her in and never come up for air. How the night we spent together shook me.

I've never been one for exercising restraint. Every second of it costs me.

I shove my hands in my pockets, where they can't reach her. "Thank you for the gift."

"About the other night," she starts at the same time.

Fuck, I'm an asshole. I should've asked how she was, but the idea of talking about the hours we spent hanging out, the times she broke apart under my hands and mouth, the long night I held her...they all make me want to lock the door and drag her down on the carpet with me until the entire department hears us.

"Are you okay?" I ask, scrutinizing her expression more closely than before. "Do you regret it?"

Her lips curve in disbelief. "Of course not." The knot in my chest eases. "And I meant it when I said my roommates won't tell. But we can't do it again, can we?"

"No. We can't."

She nods, resigned. I clear my throat.

"Olivia, I want you to know something. That was one of the worst days of my life. But thanks to you, it was also one of the best."

Her face lifts, transforming with gratitude. "I'm glad."

"And I hope I didn't screw things up with your parents."

"You didn't." She bends to pick up her school bag, flashing an expanse of smooth thigh. "I told my mom Adam and I broke up. For good this time."

My restraint cracks—a single, tragic faultline of weakness snaking through a stone foundation.

By the time she straightens, I'm across the room.

"I'm proud of you."

"Yeah?"

I nod. I want to see her tell the truth to herself and the entire world.

Whatever she sees on my face, it's something I'm going to regret because her throat works, lips parting as her gaze drops to my mouth.

"Sawyer."

Jesus. If she calls me that at work one more time...

She sneaks a look over her shoulder at the door before turning back to me. "You can fuck me if you want."

What I want is to get in so deep she can't get me out. To peel back the layers of her perfection, to strip her down and make her see she's stronger and more beautiful than even she knows. I wish she could see what I see when I look at her.

"You deserve better."

The longing on her face dissolves into frustration. "People say that, but what they mean is I should want what they choose." She shoves the hair out of her face on a long exhale. "I guess I'll see you in class."

But as she turns for the door, all I can think is how much better I feel when I'm around her. I want to be with her, but more than that, I want to see her smile. I want to *make* her smile.

Because, I realize, *she* feels better when she's with *me*.

That possibility lifts the guilt from my shoulders long enough for me to take a breath.

"Olivia." She pauses, one hand on the door handle. "I'm taking you out this weekend."

The door shuts. "Like a date?"

"A night off, far from prying eyes."

Her slim arms fold across her chest, but she's grinning every bit as much as me. "You're such a romantic."

"Friday night." I catch her lips beneath mine, inhaling her surprised breath. "Now get out of here so I can get some fucking work done."

19

OLIVIA

"Your date is here!" Jules shouts across our place.

"Already?" I curse and check my outfit.

Sawyer wouldn't tell me where we were going, but he said it was elegant. And since it's still early, I'm guessing there's some transit involved.

So I put on a red fitted D&G dress with long sleeves and a scoop neck that shows off serious cleavage. It's grown up and sexy, and though I bought it on a whim once, I've still never worn it.

I leave my hair down in soft waves. He likes touching it, and I love it when he does.

I head into the living room, half expecting to see him there. But the only person is my roommate, pouring over notes on the couch with a highlighter in her mouth.

"Some guy called from downstairs for Miss Barclay," Jules says, taking the marker from between her teeth. "Wow. You look hot."

"Thanks." My stomach tingles with excitement.

She waves toward the window. "Your prof sent an emissary."

I grab my heels and head for the door. "Let me guess. You think this is a terrible idea."

"How much do you like him?"

"A lot. Does that make it a better idea?"

"No. But it makes it more worth the risk."

I grab a jacket and wave goodbye to my roommate.

Downstairs, there's a town car nestled amongst four other cars idling near the front doors.

The second I appear, the driver steps out and rounds the car to hold my door. "Miss Barclay?"

"Yes. Thank you."

The car takes me to Lancaster's house. It's not far, but nerves spring up from nowhere.

I play with the buttons of my trench coat.
Open.
Closed.
Open.

Is this really a date, or did he mean what he said and it's just a way to blow off steam?

By the time the car pulls up to the driveway, there's no more room for second-guessing.

He's there. I catch a glimpse of him through the tinted window, and my heart kicks as the door opens.

The hand extended to help me is warm, calloused, and familiar.

Sawyer.

He's wearing designer denim with a baby blue shirt and dark jacket tailored to show off his strong shoulders and the planes of his torso. His heady, masculine scent drowns me in an instant.

"Hey," I murmur as I shift out of the car.

His gaze sweeps over me, appreciative. "My God, you're beautiful."

I inhale too fast at the expression on his face. "I could've just met you here."

"No. I wanted this moment. To see you step out of that car and know you picked out that cherry red dress for me."

So definitely a date. My insides clench in excitement.

If my reckless professor does sex well? He does dates really, *really* well.

We change vehicles, Sawyer opting to drive

his Mercedes. Once we're settled in, the town car long gone, he accelerates out onto the street.

"Now are you going to tell me where we're going?"

"No. I will tell you the drive's a couple of hours, so get comfortable."

I'm not put off at the prospect of spending two hours each way with Sawyer, if anything I'm giddy, plus I'm even more intrigued by the possibilities.

"What if I guess it?"

"Surprises are the break in the monotony of life, Olivia."

The ride is more than enjoyable. His hair is pulled back with a leather lace and I can't stop staring at his jaw and his lips.

We talk about things people dating talk about—favorite TV shows, music, hobbies. Sawyer grew up watching the reality TV series *Survivor*, which makes me snort.

"My dad said he hated it but I caught him DVR-ing it once."

My smile fades a little thinking of Lancaster. "Do you miss him?"

Sawyer glances over, serious. "Not really. Do you?"

I suck in a breath. "I think of him sometimes,

yeah. It feels strange being in a world that he's not in."

"You spent a lot of time with him."

The man beside me is close, and the one we're talking about is far away.

"Outside of class, he helped me when I needed it. Traded a few book recommendations. I told him he should get the fish, because I thought he'd appreciate something other than his students and work to love."

When I say it, I realize how that must sound to his son.

"We knew different men," Sawyer admits. "He was kind and patient with you. I never saw that side of him."

That comment lingers, echoing in my chest.

I change the subject. "When was the last time you dated?"

"More than a year ago."

"That long?" I'm surprised. "Have you had to fight women off for the last twelve months?"

It's meant as a joke but Sawyer's grip on the steering wheel tightens. "This year didn't go how I planned."

"It's not your fault your dad died. You couldn't have predicted that."

He cuts a look at me. "Not everything was his fault."

I sense there's something he's not telling me. "So who was she? The last woman you dated."

"She worked in advertising in New York."

I picture her being mature and confident and poised, and shove aside the jealousy. Tonight's about what we are, not what we aren't.

"Was it serious?"

"More on her side than on mine. She wanted things to progress. To move in together."

"Sounds crazy," I say, deadpan.

He shoots me a self-deprecating grin. "It wasn't. I get it, it's what normal people do. But I supposed I didn't grow up with normal, so by the time I could have it, I found I didn't care for it all that much."

Unlike me, Sawyer's not the kind of person who spends energy trying to fit in. He'll always stand out.

"Did you love her?"

He shakes his head. "Love is just another form of power. And unlike sex, you can never be completely consenting to someone having that kind of power over you."

"It sounds lonely."

The streetlights play over Sawyer's face as he frowns. "I've always done better on my own. I don't want anyone to depend on me. Dependence is a recipe for cruelty and disappointment.

But," he goes on, voice lifting along with his lips, "tonight will be neither cruel nor disappointing."

I thread my fingers through his and lay my head on his shoulder as we drive the rest of the way.

In the end, I don't have to guess where we're going—it becomes obvious pretty soon that New York is our destination.

When we arrive, he parks in an underground lot near Lincoln Center and walks, hand in mine, around to the entrance.

"We're going to the Koch Theater," I guess.

"When was the last time you went to the ballet?"

"Not in years."

Swan Lake.

The marquee nearly roots my feet to the carpet, but we file into the throng of elegant people.

After claiming our programs, an usher shows us to a box.

The maroon and gold splendor of the theater steals my breath. When I turn to Sawyer, he's every bit as awestruck.

"It's beautiful, isn't it?" I say.

"Yeah. It really is."

We settle into our seats and as the house lights dim, he reaches over to thread his fingers through mine like I did to him in the car.

The ballet begins with the celebration of Prince Siegfried's birthday in an old German castle, and I slip into the music and the movements. My limbs are heavy and restless at once. When the swans claim the stage for the first time, Sawyer's mouth brushes my ear.

"Are you okay?"

I nod quickly, realizing I pulled away from his touch.

My attention sticks to the ballet until intermission when the lights come up and I take a gulp of air.

The patrons are murmuring appreciatively, talking about the performance or gossiping over their weekend plans.

But Sawyer moves between me and the stage, shifting his hips back against the edge of the box.

"You're not enjoying this."

"It's not that. This was an amazing idea, it just brings back lots of memories. I wanted to dance Swan Lake since I was a little girl. I went as Odette for Halloween three years in a row." I shake my head, fisting my diamond pendant.

"And did you?"

I nod. "I was cast in a student production, and it was a dream come true. Even the hard parts. The Stars project is nothing compared to ballet rehearsals."

Sawyer's attention sharpens. "What happened?"

I drop my hand to the armrest. "My boobs came in. I stopped eating. I figured if I didn't eat, I couldn't grow, right? Of course, it's hard to dance on two hundred calories a day. It worked until I fell over in rehearsals and they took me to the emergency room. The doctors told me to eat more, but it wasn't that simple. Food was one thing I could control in a sea of things I couldn't. My mother was furious."

"Because you weren't eating."

"No. Because it didn't work."

The house lights flicker, signalling the end of intermission.

Sawyer takes my hand and tugs me to my feet, his expression dark. "Let's get out of here."

"We don't have to leave," I protest.

He takes me back out to the street, gets in his car, and drives before parking again. This time he strips out of his jacket, tossing it in the back seat before we leave the parking lot.

"The aquarium?" I ask when we stop in front of the building.

"You been?"

"Never."

A ribbon of giddy anticipation chases through me, at least until I read the hours on the front door.

"It closes in ten minutes."

Sawyer presses a kiss to my lips. "Uh-huh. Give me two."

He disappears to speak to the person on duty at the front.

I feel like I'm treading water and trying to catch up, but I don't hate it. Not even a little.

No one's ever gone to the effort Sawyer went to for me to make sure I'm having a good time.

"Let's go." He grabs my hand and I follow him into the first exhibit.

I stop next to the first tank, my feet rooted to the floor. Inside are dozens, no, hundreds, of little blue fish darting around.

"There are so many kinds and they all have their place in the ecosystem. No pressure to look or be a certain way. There's so much life. And there's room for all of it."

There's someone cleaning, and Sawyer jogs over to him, asking a few questions then clapping him on the back before returning to me.

"These are fish you'd find in the barrier reef."

"Oh really?" I bite my cheek. "In fairness, it does say that on the sign."

He's not dissuaded. "Yes, but does it say this fish can break off a piece of its tail if a predator catches it."

I laugh, delighted. "It does not."

He's like a kid. It's impossible not to get drawn in.

"The aquarium is now closing," comes a PA announcement over invisible speakers.

"Not for us," Sawyer murmurs.

We make our way from one series of tanks to the next. I gush over sea turtles and anemone as Sawyer reads the informational signs and points out the craziest fish facts.

When we pass through to another part of the aquarium, the huge round tank making me suck in a breath.

The freshly cleaned plexiglass is perfectly clear.

Beyond, half a dozen sharks circle, elegant and deadly. The beautiful creatures could rip my flesh from my bones.

"They're incredible," I murmur even as my heart hammers against my ribs, willing me to turn and run.

"Do you know why we're drawn to dangerous things?" His voice is rough silk as he flips me and presses my back to the glass.

"What makes life exciting," he goes on, "is knowing we could lose it in an instant. But it's not about putting our life in someone else's hands. It's about taking it into our own."

His warm breath tickles the skin exposed by the low neckline of my dress. My breasts strain against the material. In the corner of my eye, the sharks swim right behind me.

"You can play the game all your life only to realize winning doesn't feel as good as breaking the rules."

The thirty-foot glass wall around us, plus thousands of liters of water and fish and predators make me feel like I'm in another world. But my attention is on the man in front of me. My very own shark, with nothing between us.

I play with his hair at his nape, gathered into the leather binding. "How would you know? I don't think you've ever followed the rules."

"I tried." His throat bobs. "God knows I tried to walk away from you."

His words should be a warning. Instead, they burn away the last of my hesitation.

"Stop trying."

I bring him to me and crush his lips against mine.

His hands stroke up my bare legs and he lifts

me up against the glass. His mouth slides down to my neck, and I arch closer.

I imagine how it would feel to be his girlfriend for real.

Only with me, I want him to say *yes*.

Yes to intimacy.

Yes to love.

Yes to all of it.

The growing hardness in his pants turns me on like crazy, and he drags my panties to the side, two fingers pressing inside where I'm slick. I gasp, squirming as he probes me.

"Sawyer..." My hips rock against his hand, craving more.

The aquarium might be closed to visitors, but there are staff and cameras. We're still in public. We need to stop.

Except...

I don't want to stop.

His expression shifts as I reach for his belt, deal with the zipper on his pants. Then work them down his ass.

He sets me down, then reaches for a condom and rolls it on.

He circles my wrists, yanking them up and together so he can catch them in one strong hand.

I feel him at my entrance. When his hips

shift forward, pinning mine against the glass, he nudges me once.

Then sinks inside.

The resistance my body puts up is nothing compared to his determination.

"That's it, Cherry, take me." It's a request with a steel edge, a command wrapped in velvet.

"More."

He's so hard, thicker and longer than I'm used to.

"More."

I breathe through the intrusion, praying the fullness will give way to pleasure.

When he's all the way in, Sawyer's groan is full of awe. "Holy shit. You feel too good."

He's praising my body, but it feels like he's praising every part of me. As if I've stunned this beautiful man.

My eyes close. He's so deep, I feel him with each inhale.

It takes a moment to get used to the sensation, both of being pinned to the glass and being filled.

But after a few breaths, the stretch feels less like a burden and more like a tease.

As if there's somehow even more to experience than this.

I rock my hips, craving friction, seeking more of him the only way I can.

"I think she likes it." He's equal parts smug and intent when he pulls out, a long drag that makes me want to protest the sudden emptiness. But before I can, he's pressing back inside.

Another stroke. Not faster, but more deliberate.

Each angle of his thrust is on purpose, designed to tear a reaction from my sweat-damp body.

Each panting breath at my ear is eager, hungry to take me apart and claim his own pleasure in this frenzy.

I cry out this time.

"That's it," he rasps. "Did you know your voice changes when you're full of my cock?"

My fingers work uselessly over my head. I'm tight, torn, wrenching against his grip on me.

It's not sweet or tentative.

Sawyer *fucks* me.

My body. My heart.

If I looked in his eyes right now, he'd see how much I'm feeling in this moment. How utterly ruined he's making me with every touch, every stroke.

Our noises echo off the glass.

"Let go." His voice near my cheek makes me shiver.

I can't tell if the words are his or mine until he says them again. "Olivia, sweetheart. Let go."

His lips brush my ear and I tremble because it's gentle and personal. As if he knows exactly what's going through my head, as if without seeing my face he's aware of everything in my body, my mind.

Which is impossible.

But when his grip on my wrists relaxes a degree, his other arm wraps around my body to hold me closer while his thrusts slow, deepen.

Oh God.

I turn my face to the side, and he takes advantage. Lips and teeth and tongue devour every inch of my exposed throat and chest.

It's close, I'm close, and in a second the pleasure in me tightens into a ripe bud that's about to burst.

There's nothing I can do to stop it.

My eyes fly open.

A shark with bared teeth swims inches from my head.

The jolt of fear only adds to the sensations. I clench hard around him, pleasure colliding with sharp pain that has every inch of me tightening right down to my toes.

"Fuck yes. Keep coming." Sawyer's voice transforms, the softness turning into a growl.

The dirty rasp makes me tremble, turning each ripple of release into its own earthquake.

In another few strokes, he tenses, and his groan in my ear is the sexiest sound I've ever heard.

We're not in New York, dressed in expensive clothes, at the aquarium he bribed his way into. We're on the edge of a thrilling wilderness I never knew existed. One that would've terrified me before him, but now, I want to move further into that tantalizing unknown.

I would give anything to keep feeling this way, but I'm desperately afraid nothing will ever measure up.

20

OLIVIA

"**D**oes it work?" Sawyer asks in the lab Monday.

"Of course." I sound more confident than I feel.

"We have one week until qualifying. It has to," presses Madison.

Around classes, the four of us have been putting in a ton of hours on this.

We've had issues with hardware, with code, with design. Last night, our invention actually performed the way it was supposed to.

Our professor crosses his arms, his firm mouth pursed. "Let's see it."

We demo the robot, putting it through a set of lifting, grasping, and manipulation tasks—first using a tennis ball, then a small spiral notebooks, a tougher object to pick up and work with.

I'm holding my breath as each hurdle is passed.

We're being judged by a different Sawyer than the one I've slept with and joked with and played JENGA with. This man is our professor and his opinion matters.

"Why did you choose three joints?" he asks, his attention laser-focused.

"Madison pointed out that we need to trade off range against risk of failure." She looks at me in surprise as my hands twist together behind my back. "But we made some improvements to the design and materials this week to ensure it's robust."

Adam and Royce talk with Sawyer while Madison comes over.

"He's decided to at least pretend to be a mentor," she comments. "What changed?"

"No idea." But my gaze lingers on Sawyer. His expression is intent as he listens to Royce, even though he stiffens when Adam leans over to weigh in.

His dress shirt clings to his shoulders and arms. The belt resting above his lean hips makes my throat dry as I remember undoing it.

"You can play the game all your life only to

realize winning doesn't feel as good as breaking the rules."

It's been harder to hide our relationship since our date.

Not only was the sex totally hot, but the entire night, Sawyer made me feel treasured. Instead of expecting me to behave a certain way, he tuned in to what I wanted. I loved every second with him.

Thank goodness we don't have a lot of time together in front of other people on campus. But when we are, we need to be more careful.

We will.

"Hard at work, I see."

We all turn to see the dean smiling from the doorway.

"You'll be pleased to know there has been external interest in your project. I wanted to see what the talk was about." He puffs his chest, surveying the robot on the table.

My teammates and I exchange surprised looks.

"Of course. They've made significant progress in limited time," Sawyer says smoothly.

"Good. The five of you will be traveling to compete in Manhattan. I trust you'll represent the school impeccably."

"Four," I correct. "Faculty advisors don't participate until finals."

I can't imagine spending an entire weekend around Sawyer in front of Adam, Royce, and Madison. If they had any idea what was going on, they'd freak out—Adam because he's my ex, Royce because this project means everything to him, and Madison because she already thinks I get special treatment.

The dean waves a hand. "Nonsense. We need to show everyone we're supporting our team. Professor Redmond will attend the weekend's activities, too."

Sawyer's gaze locks with mine, and I see the same expression reflected on his face.

This is bad.

21

OLIVIA

I throw myself into working on our project for the last week before regionals.

My dance class is the only relief, and even as I'm teaching the guppies, I'm thinking about the weekend with anticipation and dread.

Friday, we head to New York on the train. The four of us ride in coach, with Sawyer in business.

I remind myself it's a good thing I don't have the chance to sneak looks at him the entire trip.

"Our own rooms," Royce comments as we roll our bags in the front doors of the Hilton. "Department's sparing no expense."

I roll my eyes.

"Get a good night's sleep," Sawyer instructs.

"The competition is tomorrow morning. You can unwind at the reception after."

"If we get through," I point out.

"Who's keeping the robot?" Madison asks.

"I will," Adam says.

"Don't use it to jerk off," Royce warns.

"Just cause she doesn't like you the way she likes me..."

"Adam. I can't believe I'm saying this"—Sawyer looks pained—"but do not stick your dick anywhere near that robot."

When we go to check in, the hotel staff says there's a mistake. "We only have four rooms."

"You girls room together," Royce suggests.

Madison and I might kill each other.

"Or Liv can room with me." Adam reaches for my bag.

"No," Sawyer and I say at once.

Madison and Royce exchange a long look, and she finally says, "It's fine. I'll room with Olivia."

We go up to our rooms. The four are on the same floor, two on each side.

Our room is next to Sawyer's.

Of course.

I feel his gaze on me as Madison and I swipe the keycard and let ourselves in.

Once we're are inside, she flops down on the bed by the window.

I grab my phone and send a text to Sawyer.

Liv: We've got this. We can crush the competition and be completely casual around each other.

Dots appear seconds later.

Unknown: You'll be pleased to know that Daniel is taking his job of feeding the fish this weekend very seriously.

The photo accompanying the text is Sawyer's friend giving a thumbs-up in front of the tank. I'd forgotten about the fish this weekend, but I love that Sawyer didn't.

Unknown: P.S. Your confidence is sexy as fuck.

"You ever get the feeling that it's easier for guys?"

I drop the phone on the bed, surprised Madison's voluntarily speaking to me. "Relationships or school?"

"Everything."

I start unpacking. "Did you watch *The Queen's Gambit* on Netflix?"

"Yes. In two days. She drank and got high to deal with her obsessive chess drive and the guys around her."

"I get that," I say as I finish hanging clothes in the closet and turn back.

"You want to raid the minibar and pound pills? Olivia Barclay, bad girl." Madison pulls out some weed that has my brows lifting.

I leave the phone on my bed and follow Madison out the screen door.

Her joint is already lit, the pungent smoke drifting up from the end when I lean over the glass railing next to her.

"It's only a little," she says in response to my look. "It'll help take the pressure off. Otherwise I won't be able to sleep."

She holds out the joint and with a moment's hesitation I accept.

"We have to make our own way," she tells me. "Guys want to help us, but they don't really."

I inhale, the smoke going to my head. "They're not all assholes."

"Even if they don't think they are, they are. It's not an ethical problem, it's a self-awareness problem. Take Adam. He doesn't think he's a dick. Or Royce. Or Redmond."

I pass the joint back and wrap my sweater around me against the cool evening air. "Professor Redmond's nothing like Adam. Neither is Royce, for that matter."

She shoots me a "get real" look. "Everyone wants Professor Redmond, and he's untouchable. You think he likes you, but he likes the power."

I glance toward the next balcony—*his*.

I wonder what he's doing tonight. There's no sign of him, and when we finally head back into the room, he hasn't texted either. So, I type out a message and hit send.

Liv: I'm glad you're here with us. As hard as it is to look at you and know we can't do anything, I'd rather have you standing next to me.

After brushing my teeth and changing into pajamas, there's still no response.

Liv: Good night, Sawyer.

22

———

SAWYER

"Sawyer Redmond," calls a familiar voice across the lobby bar.

I look up from my computer where I'm reading the business news. Tate strolls over to claim a stool next to me at the bar, his suit wrinkled. "It's not fair. I got in from an overnight flight from Tokyo, and you look like a billboard. Leave something for the rest of us."

"Plenty of people would agree the world would be better without me. Intellectually. Morally." I take in his neatly trimmed hair, tugging on the ends of my own. "Even esthetically."

He orders a drink, smirking. "Did my call to your dean resolve the politics you were hoping to avoid?"

"In a way." It also resulted in me being here this weekend, but I don't say that.

"Some days, I'm not sure why I agreed to go into business with you."

"Because I have vision and you have execution."

Tate's a decade older, and we've always been competitors. Except when I left my company, I needed to find a new direction. A better one.

"And you're good at getting what you want."

"Am I?" I scan the lobby as he gets his drink and takes a sip. "If I'd gotten my way, we would already be in business together."

"But the world also takes time to forget. What happened earlier this year was unfortunate."

My hand clenches my glass. The anger and guilt over those events still boils deep inside, overcooked resentment left to simmer for months until it's black and sticky.

"Those events weren't my fault. Yet I was left to pay the steepest price."

"You're not the only person still hung up on how things ended with your former business partner, which is why we agreed to a cooling off period first. You need to avoid any indiscretions —real or perceived. Plus, we agreed it looks good on our future company to have you at such an esteemed institution in the interim. What's so bad about being at Russell? Innovative colleagues, dedicated staff, bright students who worship you. I took a look at your team," he goes on. "Two men, two women. How egalitarian."

His words are mild but there's an edge beneath.

"Madison is ambitious," I start. "Olivia is talented and hardworking."

I think about the girl upstairs who's been turning me inside out.

Our date last week changed our relationship—there's no questioning it, no denying it. It wasn't only the sex at the aquarium.

Every time I push her, she opens up. Whether she knows it or not, she's opening me up, too.

Each day I spend with her, I want more.

"The events of last year linger like a bad smell, rubbing off on anyone who comes in contact with them," Tate says under his breath. "I'm not out to get you. I want to help you."

That doesn't soothe my frustration.

I've never done well with warnings. But he's right, she shouldn't be any of my business.

If anyone were to find out, the future I've worked for could be over before it began.

But I'm not willing to walk away from her.

Which means I need to talk to her—to be

honest about why I'm here, and what our relationship could cost me.

I glance at my phone to reread the message that came in an hour ago.

Cherry: I'm glad you're here with us. As hard as it is to look at you and know we can't do anything, I'd rather have you standing next to me.

My fingers itch to respond. But before I came down here, I glanced out the patio doors of my room to see her outside smoking a joint and having a conversation with her unwanted roommate.

She's a student. She deserves to be a kid and enjoy this experience with people her own age.

Another message lights up the screen.

Cherry: Good night, Sawyer.

"You sure you still want to go into business with me? Sounds like you're getting into this whole professor thing," Tate asks.

I toss my drink back, shoving the phone away. "I've never been more certain."

23

OLIVIA

After taking turns in the shower, Madison and I head downstairs for breakfast.

I read over the rules last night.

Every team has five minutes to present their design to the judges, including their aspirations for what would be completed if their team is chosen to proceed to nationals.

The panel casts their votes, and the top third of teams will continue to the next round.

It's not until I spot the crowd of students and judges and sponsors that my stomach does a little flip like it used to before a dance performance.

This is a big deal.

My fingers wrap around my necklace.

I want to do well today. Qualifying matters. It's a chance to prove I can contribute in my own way, that the work I've put in this semester and in recent years to this major my parents wanted no part of is paying off.

Only succeeding won't come down to my well-rehearsed performance of someone else's choreography, but to our entire team's ideas and capabilities.

I finally got a message from Sawyer this morning that came in overnight.

Unknown: Sorry. Ran into an old friend and time got away.

There's no *Cherry*, no *Olivia*, and it's funny how the simple absence of either makes me wish he hadn't texted at all.

I'm sipping my coffee and eating pineapple when Adam and Royce come down and claim chairs across the table from us. They're arguing over some comic book Royce brought with him.

My gaze drifts across the restaurant to see Sawyer, looking handsome and remote in a dark jacket and jeans.

"Redmond," a male voice calls over the hum of chatter.

Sawyer pulls up a few feet from the table as a

tall man in a suit with a head of neat, graying hair approaches.

The man grins, clapping our professor on the back. "Surprised to see you up this early after last night."

"Tate's a colleague," Sawyer explains. "We're going into business together."

"If he can keep his nose clean."

What does that mean?

"You're lucky to have him," Tate goes on. "This man is one of the brightest minds of his generation."

"Are you here with a team?" I ask when Sawyer introduces the man.

"No. My company is sponsoring the competition." He lifts his brows, waiting for a name.

"Olivia," I supply.

The man's attention lingers on me. "Olivia. Pleased to meet you."

Sawyer's grip tightens on his plate. "See you around, Tate."

"No doubt. With luck, we can toast at the reception tonight on a job well done."

As his friend departs, I wish I could ask him what's wrong, but there's no time, or place.

"You're ready?" Sawyer asks.

We nod.

"There's a faculty supervisor meeting soon. I'll catch up with you after."

I stare after him as he leaves, wishing I could ask him what the hell is going on.

"So the demos start at ten," I say to the team, pulling out the agenda. "The top fifteen teams get through to the second round. It says we need to have the bot in the room by nine"—I skim the text—"or we'll be disqualified. But Adam took care of that."

Instead of a quick confirmation, silence meets my ears.

I look up. "Adam? You brought the bot down before you came to breakfast. Right?"

He and Royce exchange a look.

"*Shit.*"

We race upstairs.

But the wheeled platform is stuck.

"Let's carry it."

Royce and Adam heft the robot to the elevator.

It opens on the trade show floor and they look around at the competition. "There're a lot of teams."

"It'll be fine," Adam retorts.

The door starts to close.

"Guys!" I shout as I lunge for the open door button.

I'm too late, and the door shuts on the final two sections of the mechanical arm.

"What the hell!" Madison punches Royce in the arm.

Adam holds up both hands. "Chill. It's fine."

Both sections fall off.

24

OLIVIA

We wheel the robot into position and I'm already sweating.

Sawyer's still in meetings, plus this is our responsibility.

I need some of the textbooks lined up next to my desk at home. Or a couple of hours with my phone, pouring over videos and articles.

We have neither.

Think, dammit.

Around the room, other teams are practicing with their projects, polishing and finessing. They look capable and competent.

Our decapitated submission stares listlessly back at me.

"Okay, so we can reattach these joints. It's the only way." I lift the final segment. "Royce?"

He nods. "But we need to resolder this." He points to one of the wires responsible for ensuring our commands get translated into movement.

I look up at Adam.

"I brought tools, but we're out of copper solder."

"Madison?" I ask, desperate.

She frowns at the machine.

"We've busted our asses for this," I say. "And it's not ending now. Adam, I know you want to prove you're good at this. Royce, it's your future. Madison, show all the teams with guys that we're better."

She rolls her eyes. "Team Double V."

"That's not our name," Royce groans.

"We can renegotiate it after we get this fixed."

There's no time to go out and buy a replacement.

So I search the room, trying to spot another group who might have what we're looking for.

A team of four guys a few spots down from us also has a robotics project.

I grab Madison and drag her with me.

"Hey. Do you guys have any copper solder?"

"Yeah," a tall, freckled guy with glasses responds.

Relief has my chest collapsing. "Amazing. Can we use some? It would be a lifesaver."

"You didn't bring extra?" he laughs. "Have you ever entered an engineering competition before?"

"No," I admit. "Next time we'll bring backups of everything. But for today, we'd be beyond grateful if you'd share yours."

They argue internally, a hushed debate I can't make out.

"How grateful?" another guy breaks their huddle to ask, pointedly checking me out.

"Tell me he didn't ask me to trade sex for solder," I whisper to Madison.

"Yeah, I wish I could."

But unless I do something, our shot will be over before it's begun.

As intimidating as this room is, the prospect of becoming a real, working engineer has never felt closer.

My hands reach up to unclasp my diamond necklace. I try not to look at how the gem catches the light as I hold it out.

"I'll give you this. It's real."

They exchange looks.

Say no, part of me shouts.

"Deal."

Madison is strangely quiet as we head back with our prize, a few dollars of cheap materials.

"Do we want to know what you both did to get this?" Royce asks dryly.

Adam's crouched next to the robot, but he flicks his gaze up and immediately spots my missing necklace.

I hand him the solder. "Just fix it."

"And the final team to qualify...Russell University."

We all sag in relief against our table.

"Fuck yeah we did." Adam holds up a hand, and even I can't deny him the high-five.

"How does it feel?" Madison asks.

"Better than dancing *Swan Lake*," I say.

"What do you think, Professor Redmond?" Royce calls.

I turn to see Sawyer, hands in his pockets, smirking. "It's passable."

"Passable? Pretty sure you owe us a beer," Adam comments.

"You could win the entire competition and I will never buy you a beer."

I bite my cheek, trying to picture Sawyer doing anything for Adam.

We all head to lunch together and I drop into a seat next to Adam. Madison and Royce start bickering.

Moments later, something brushes my knee under the table.

Sawyer. Awareness lifts the hairs on my neck.

He's taken the chair on my other side, and his leg rests against mine.

I want to close my eyes at the feel of it.

"Olivia. I'd like a word after lunch."

The fact that he's asking in front of the others is bold, and my hand fists under the table.

His gaze hits me square in the chest—the confidence, pride, admiration.

"Of course, Professor."

I want to bask in it. Instead, I take a sip of my water.

"You gave up your necklace to fix the robot, didn't you?"

Adam's voice tears my attention away.

"It's not a big deal."

"It is a big deal. You got it for dancing *Swan Lake*. Not to mention it's probably worth what, five grand? Ten? I didn't know you were so serious about this, Liv."

"Well, I am."

I feel Sawyer's eyes in my back.

"Excuse me," he says. "I need to go do something."

"You don't want to talk?"

He turns that over. "Later."

Before I can protest, he's gone.

Following lunch, the agenda is filled with informational sessions and meetings.

On the way to the elevator at the end of the day, I run into Sawyer's friend in the lobby.

"Tate," he says warmly as I try to remember his name.

I smile. "Right."

"I heard you had to make some last-minute repairs."

"There was a challenge in transporting our project," I say. "I wasn't about to let this go up in flames."

"Well, if you win the competition, you'll have a million dollars. You could get a job working for someone else, or you could invest the prize in R&D to build your company. Set up shop in the Valley, or wherever you want. I could give you advice on that, at the right time."

"Thank you." The idea of going into business with Royce, Adam, and Madison feels like a world away, but setting up a company based on the work we're doing is an exciting possibility.

"You have good advice in the interim. Sawyer's the smartest man I know."

I'm still riding the high of success, and can't resist teasing. "So why is he working with us instead of with you?"

Tate's nostrils flare, his smile tightening. "Because even smart people do stupid things."

He continues on his way and I'm left staring after him.

25

OLIVIA

"Cute outfit," I tell Madison as she turns in the mirror with her blue silk jumpsuit.

"Thanks. You too."

I pat down my cocktail dress. I pulled my hair back in a sleek ponytail and applied my eyeliner darker than I'd normally do it for a school event. "I don't look like a stripper?"

She ducks her face, guilt flickering across her expression. "You know that what you did today was really decent."

"I'm glad we got through." I square my shoulders, ignoring how bare my neck feels without the good luck charm I've worn for years.

My phone buzzes, and I check it.

Unknown: You were fantastic today.

The sadness about my necklace evaporates. I grin and type back.

Liv: I accept payment in the form of lavish praise and orgasms. Speaking of which, you wanted to meet up.

Unknown: Mhmm. I'll find you at the reception.

"Listen, I'm really sorry about the Velvet video. I did post it, but it wasn't my idea."

Madison interrupts my thoughts and I straighten in surprise. "Then whose was it?"

She only shakes her head.

I'm not sure what to say, but I'm grateful for the ceasefire in our hostilities.

So we head downstairs for the reception and join the crowd of students, faculty and industry people milling about the ballroom.

We're on a different floor than the day's earlier activities, and it's strange how now that the competition is done for the day, everyone is friendlier.

Royce looks extra handsome tonight, and he watches every move Madison makes.

"What's up with you and Royce?" I murmur to her.

She rolls her eyes. "Nothing. And there won't be. Even if we were good together, I don't want anything to get in the way of this project. It matters too much."

But when a captain of another team introduces himself, she allows herself to be sucked into conversation.

"You ever seen *The Queen's Gambit*?" he starts. "It must be hard for women surrounded by men."

"Buy me a drink."

"It's an open bar."

She blinks at him and he leaps into action.

I'm still smiling when Sawyer comes up behind me. "You look stunning."

"And I'm wearing your favorite underwear."

"Which are?"

I focus on the room in front of me despite the heat of his attention. "None."

The soft noise behind me might be a groan. "Olivia...Meet me in the North stairwell at eleven."

Does he want to hook up here, at the hotel? It's insane. But maybe we can find somewhere out of sight. If I'm lucky everyone will be drunk like after Fall Ball, and our absence won't be noticed.

Sawyer's attention is stolen by some men in suits, and I admire him a moment before turning away.

"Excuse me," I ask one of the guys from another team, "do you know where the women's bathroom is?"

They exchange a look. "Do we look like we know where the women's bathroom is?"

The laughter follows me as I turn on my heel and leave the ballroom.

I search through the halls, and after few moments, I find the bathroom. It's empty when I slip into a stall.

As I reach for toilet paper, two voices enter.

"...that contract went to Ajax. No one saw it coming."

"No one? Come on. It's been a year since their Series B funding."

They must be sponsors—they sound older than students, plus most students don't keep up on industry happenings.

I tune them out until one of them gasps. "Oh my God. Did you see him here? He brought a team. I'm shocked he's in public."

"Who?"

"Sawyer Redmond."

"Why did he leave New York?"

"He was screwing his partner's nineteen-year-old daughter. They couldn't have him in the company after that."

The blood drains from my head.

When they leave, I trip out of the stall. My hands brace on the cool marble sink.

It can't be true. Sawyer wouldn't have had an affair with a teenager.

But the knot in my chest twists tighter.

He was so angry when he learned I was his student—I thought it was because he knew we couldn't keep seeing each other, but what if it's something else?

Plus he's been tight-lipped about why he left his company. And Tate was cryptic about why he's not working with Sawyer now.

Is that why he was looking at me suspiciously? He's worried it's happening again?

Sweat beads at my neck.

No. Sawyer sees me. He cares about me.

But if I'm not special, if I'm just a type for him...I can't bear it.

Outside, I grab another drink.

Then another.

Somehow I make it back up to my room.

I pass out on the bed until a pounding on my door wakes me.

"Olivia!" Sawyer's voice outside my door is insistent. "Are you in there?"

I roll off the bed, tug my dress down and stumble across the floor. The clock says it's nearly midnight.

I jerk the door open to find Sawyer, shirt rolled up to his elbows, hair wild, expression tight with concern. "You didn't meet me. I couldn't find—"

"Did you leave New York because you were fucking your partner's teenage daughter?"

The words are shards of glass in my throat.

I wait for him to say I'm crazy. But when his nostrils flare, his jaw clenching, the hurt slices deeper.

"Jesus, Olivia." His head drops back.

"Did you?"

"You seem to think so."

He's calm. How is he this calm, when it feels like everything is crashing down around me?

Sawyer shoves a hand through his hair. "You're talking about a time before I came to Russell. Before I met you."

He's the first person in the world who made me feel like he saw me for me. If this is true... then Madison is right and it's all about the power for him, and it was never about me at all.

My eyes burn. "That's why you left your company on bad terms you refuse to talk about, isn't it? It's why you came here—not only because your dad died, but because you had to leave the city."

He doesn't deny it.

Doesn't do anything but look at me with pity and regret.

"God, I'm so stupid." It takes everything in me to force out the words. "I cared about you, and this was...what? A game? A challenge?"

The anguish on his face hardens into an unreadable mask. "No."

"Then what was it?" I choke out.

He doesn't answer.

The dinging sound from down the hall might as well be from another world.

All I hear is the blood rushing in my ears.

All I feel is agony, because the heart I didn't realize I gave him before now is breaking.

"We're done, Sawyer," I whisper. "No more dates. No more sex. No more texting. This thing between us...it's over."

His expression contorts, his handsome face twisting with denial, then disbelief.

Movement in the corner of my damp eyes rips my gaze away.

Madison stands frozen by the elevator, both hands over her mouth.

She heard every word.

Thank you for reading *Crave*! I hope you loved Sawyer and Olivia's story.

CAN SAWYER DEFY HIS PAST TO WIN OLIVIA BACK WHEN HIS SECRETS CATCH UP TO THEM? FIND OUT IN COLLIDE...

Read a short excerpt below

I'm staring at Sawyer like he's from another planet.

One full of beautiful, reckless men in tuxedos.

But there's only one who makes my palms sweat and my designer cocktail dress tighten as I struggle to breathe.

"Dance with me," he murmurs.

Is he joking?

"We're in the middle of a fundraiser," I say, my heart accelerating.

His mouth twitches. "If we were in private you'd say yes?"

Damn him.

My family is here.

All of New York is here.

I shake myself. "No. I don't want to dance with you."

"You weren't having a good time with *him*," my professor says smoothly.

"And you think I'll have a better time with you?" I counter.

Sure, the guy I had been dancing with, the son of one of my mother's friends who's at Columbia, was talking my ear off even before he tried to feel me up.

He also left the second Sawyer cut in.

On stage, my reckless professor seemed determined to prove a point. My parents were appalled by the idea of calling out a room full of rich donors, especially if it required spilling your guts to do it.

I didn't think it was crude.

It was brave.

"Yes. Because you don't have to pretend with me."

The truth of it vibrates down to my bones.

Tonight, I wanted to enjoy the evening with my family. I was starting to believe this life wasn't so bad—until my dad reinforced this is all an act, and my future rests in the balance.

The only person who's not acting here is the man in front of me.

Sawyer's waiting for me to respond, and now, with the music and the darkened lights and everything that's happened tonight, I force the words from my lips. "We can't do this."

"Here or at all?" He steps closer, his scent flooding my senses as his body crowds me.

"Both."

His palm is warm and rough as it clasps mine, his eyes flashing with urgency and emotion I don't dare name.

"Noted," he whispers.

End of Sample
To continue reading, be sure to pick up *Collide* at your favorite retailer.

BOOKS BY PIPER LAWSON

FOR A FULL LIST PLEASE GO TO
PIPERLAWSONBOOKS.COM/BOOKS

KING OF THE COURT SERIES

*After being dumped and losing my job the same week,
the last thing my broken heart needs is a rebound.*

A steamy, grumpy sunshine sports romance featuring
a woman down on her luck, a star basketball player
with a filthy mouth, and a connection neither of
them can deny.

OFF-LIMITS SERIES

*Turns out the beautiful man from the club is my new
professor... But he wasn't when he kissed me.*

Off-Limits is a forbidden age gap college romance
series. Find out what happens when the beautiful
man from the club is Olivia's hot new professor.

WICKED SERIES

*Rockstars don't chase college students. But Jax Jamieson
never followed the rules.*

Wicked is a new adult rock star series full of nerdy
girls, hot rock stars, pet skunks, and ensemble casts
you'll want to be friends with forever.

RIVALS SERIES

At seventeen, I offered Tyler Adams my home, my life, my heart. He stole them all.

Rivals is an angsty new adult series. Fans of forbidden romance, enemies to lovers, friends to lovers, and rock star romance will love these books.

ENEMIES SERIES

I sold my soul to a man I hate. Now, he owns me.

Enemies is an enthralling, explosive romance about an American DJ and a British billionaire. If you like wealthy, royal alpha males, enemies to lovers, travel or sexy romance, this series is for you!

TRAVESTY SERIES

My best friend's brother grew up. Hot.

Travesty is a steamy romance series following best friends who start a fashion label from NYC to LA. It contains best friends brother, second chances, enemies to lovers, opposites attract and friends to lovers stories. If you like sexy, sassy romances, you'll love this series.

PLAY SERIES

I know what I want. It's not Max Donovan. To hell with his money, his gaming empire, and his joystick.

Play is an addictive series of standalone romances with slow burn tension, delicious banter, office romance and unforgettable characters. If you like smart, quirky, steamy enemies-to-lovers, contemporary romance, you'll love Play.

MODERN ROMANCE SERIES

When your rich, handsome best friend asks you to be his fake girlfriend? Say no.

Modern Romance is a smart, sexy series of contemporary romances following a set of female friends running a relationship marketing company in NYC. If you enjoy hot guys who treat their families like gold, fun antics, dirty talk, real characters, steamy scenes, badass heroines and smart banter, you'll love the Modern Romance series.

ABOUT THE AUTHOR

Piper Lawson is a WSJ and USA Today bestselling author of smart and steamy romance.

She writes women who follow their dreams, best friends who know your dirty secrets and love you anyway, and complex heroes you'll fall hard for.

Piper lives in Canada with her tall and brilliant husband. She's a sucker for dark eyes, dark coffee, and dark chocolate.

For a complete reading list, visit
www.piperlawsonbooks.com/books

Subscribe to Piper's VIP email list
www.piperlawsonbooks.com/subscribe

amazon.com/author/piperlawson

bookbub.com/authors/piper-lawson

instagram.com/piperlawsonbooks

facebook.com/piperlawsonbooks

goodreads.com/piperlawson

ACKNOWLEDGMENTS

I've been longing to write a college romance for YEARS. While I have a couple of stories set there (Schooled and A Love Song for Rebels), it's never been enough to satisfy me. I love the thrills of freedom and first-time-adulthood...the friends and the pressures and the triumphs.

Sawyer and Liv wouldn't have happened without the support of my awesome readers, including my ARC team. You ladies provide endless enthusiasm, cheerleading, and help spreading the word. I could NOT do it without you, and it would be a lot less fun to try.

An extra shoutout to everyone who read early, commented, brainstormed and hand-held to make this the best story it can be. Tal, Sara, Suzanne, and Tina: thank you for parsing ALL the pages, for catching typos, and for identifying gems of opportunity ripe for polishing. (You all owe me some kidneys.) Plus Maddie, Beth, Anna,

Nicola, Annette, your help with the 1.0 version of this story, Tease Me, set the foundation for this entire world.

Thank you Regina Wamba for the perfect image.

Becca Mysoor, thank you for knowing the characters in my head better than I do, and proving it every day. Erica Russikoff, thank you for polishing, cheerleading and catching all the little things.

Thank you Dani Sanchez for your sage advice and for helping my stories find their way to readers who'll cherish them like I do.

And Annette Brignac and Michelle Clay... I don't know how I published a sentence before you. Don't ever leave me.

Thank you all from the bottom of my heart. The best part of author life is having YOU in it.

Love always,
Piper